Claudia rose slowly from the chair and faced him *from* with her arms folded.

"Do you truly think me mad?" she asked softly, nervous as to what his answer might be.

His brows furrowed. Finally he sighed and shook his head. "No, I don't think that at all. It's just that I don't know what to think of you. You seem to do things without any forethought or regard for your own safety." He paused and held his hands up in a helpless gesture. "Frankly, Claudia, you worry me. I fear that the next time I find you, you'll be hurt, or I'll hear you've been sent back to America because your grandfather found out what you've been doing."

Her eyes widened with anxiety. "You're not going to tell him, are you? If he finds out, he'll take me to Scotland and marry me off to some burly highlander with bad manners. And I can't—"

Cameron pressed his finger over her lips. "What are you talking about? What highlander?"

She grabbed his hand and moved it from her mouth. "*Any* highlander—it doesn't matter! He's always vexed with me, Cameron, and if he knows I've dressed like a boy and risked my life to look for my—well, look for someone—he'll marry me off, and I'll have to live in the mountains where it snows all the time and—"

"Claudia, if you will calm down—"

"No, no! You must not—"

He kissed her again.

KIMBERLEY COMEAUX is a pastor's wife who wears many hats, including choir director, women's ministries leader, and Web designer for her church. Her first love, however, remains dreaming up and writing inspirational romances for the wonderful Heartsong readers! She lives in Cajun, Louisiana, with her husband, Brian; teenage son, Tyler; and their two dogs.

Books by Kimberley Comeaux

HEARTSONG PRESENTS

Don't miss out on any of our super romances. Write to us at the following address for information on our newest releases and club information.

Heartsong Presents Readers' Service
PO Box 721
Uhrichsville, OH 44683

Or visit www.heartsongpresents.com

A Gentleman's Kiss

Kimberley Comeaux

Heartsong Presents

To my dearest friend since eighth grade, Julie Canterbury Everett. When I needed inspiration for Claudia and Helen's friendship, I thought of you.

And to my aunts, Judy Lamb and Alicia Nichols, who are always full of fun and a big supporters of my writing.

A note from the Author:
I love to hear from my readers! You may correspond with me by writing:

Kimberley Comeaux
Author Relations
PO Box 721
Uhrichsville, OH 44683

ISBN 1-59310-880-X

A GENTLEMAN'S KISS

one

London, England, 1816

"What do you think Lady Exeter would do if I tied my skirts and scurried up that large oak over there?" Lady Claudia Baumgartner asked her friend Helen, the Duchess of Northingshire, as they strolled through Hyde Park.

"Hmm." Helen tapped her finger on her rosy cheek. They both eyed Lady Exeter, who was dressed from head to toe in green ruffles and feathers. If anyone could make or break one's favor with the *ton*, which represented all of English noble society, it would be this formidable woman. "Well, after she had finished huffing and puffing with acute vexation, she would snap out her green-feathered fan, wave it toward you, and declare you mad and unfit for the title of Marchioness of Moreland!"

Claudia laughed. "It might be worth my reputation just to witness her vexation," she said, teasing.

"My dear friend, you can witness it on any number of occasions." Helen smiled. "All Lady Exeter has to do is see me on the arm of my beloved husband, and she lets everyone in our vicinity know how put out about the marriage she is."

Claudia glanced at Helen. Although her tone had remained pleasant, Claudia worried that it still caused her friend pain whenever she was belittled. English society did not look favorably on those who married above their stations as Helen had when she married the Duke of Northingshire.

Claudia started to apologize for mentioning it, but Helen stopped her.

"Do not look so bothered, Claudia. I'm fine, really. I am concerned about you, though."

Claudia was taken aback. "Me? Whatever for?"

"You seem so lonely away from your home in America. I keep thinking that if you made a good match it might alleviate some of your melancholy."

Claudia smiled at her friend. "Just because marriage agrees with you, it does not follow it would agree with me, as well. Besides, I have not found a man in all of England I like enough to consider a match." She looked around the large wooded park at the handsomely dressed ladies and gentlemen and sighed. "Besides your husband, and possibly the Thornton brothers, there is no one I would think manly enough to attract me. Most of these gentlemen are. . .too soft," she finished.

Helen giggled. "You are just used to those rugged American and Indian men like Sam. To tell you the truth, Sam scared me to death when he kept trying to trade his horses for me. Nothing seems civilized over there!"

Claudia smiled at her. She remembered the time Helen spent in Louisiana as a companion to Claudia's younger sister, Josie, when she met their neighbor Sam, a Choctaw Indian. Their lives *were* similar in some ways—Helen, a farmer's daughter, had left her comfortable life to live with her husband in the sometimes harsh world of the ton, and Claudia had left her family, friends, and country to live with her grandfather in a land so different from her own.

For that reason Claudia was experiencing a twinge of melancholy. She'd received a letter from her sister the day before, and it reminded her of how homesick she was for her native Louisiana.

When she had first heard that her grandfather, the Marquis of Moreland, had asked her to come and live with him and become heir to his title, Claudia had jumped at the chance. After all, she had always dreamed of what it must be like to wear beautiful dresses and attend balls and parties during the season.

And, too, it was a chance to redeem her father's name and heritage that had been damaged when he had married the daughter of the marquis's butler. Claudia's grandfather had disowned him, cutting him off with only a small inheritance from his mother. Left with few options Claudia's parents, Robert and Imogene Baumgartner, fled to America and established a plantation in south Louisiana not far from New Orleans. It was there Claudia and her sister, Josie, were born and reared on the Golden Bay Plantation, surrounded by swamps and bayous, with members of the Choctaw Indian tribe as their playmates.

In the two years she had been in England, however, nothing had been as she had imagined. Her grandfather was gruff and distant, often causing Claudia to feel alone. The balls were also a letdown. For though they were grand, she had so many rules and restrictions placed upon her that she had no time left to enjoy herself.

At first, the ton had labeled her a rustic and an oddity because of her accent and lack of graces. But the prince regent took an immediate liking to her when she met him and labeled her "an original." After that she was invited to all the parties, and every eligible gentleman clamored for her affections. In fact, she was often so overwhelmed by people, she wished she could go back to being unpopular.

"So how is your search going for your mother's father?" Helen asked, pulling Claudia from her musings.

"My grandfather still will not speak of him, and he has forbidden the servants to tell me anything either," she said with a sigh. She'd been searching for her other grandfather, George Canterbury, since she'd arrived in England, but the only news she'd managed to procure was concerning the marquis. Lord Moreland had terminated her grandfather Canterbury's employment when he'd become aware of Robert and Imogene's relationship. "I'm not even sure he's alive, Helen. Perhaps I am wasting my time."

Helen took her hand and gave it a squeeze before releasing it. "Nonsense! I have told my husband about it, and he has been making inquiries on your behalf. Between the three of us we will find him," Helen assured her.

Claudia smiled at Helen and silently sent up a prayer of thanks to God for sending her a friend so loyal and true. "Please give him my sincere thanks," she said earnestly. "If anyone can find out anything, I know North can," she continued, using the duke's nickname.

"Of course he can," Helen agreed.

"Once I find my other grandfather, perhaps I'll be in better spirits, and you won't have to try to match me with every suitable man in London," she teased.

"Not every man, Claudia—just the right one," Helen suddenly stopped, and her breath caught. "Of course! *He* would be perfect."

Claudia studied her friend's awestruck expression warily. "What are you talking about?"

Helen made a discreet movement with her hand toward the bridge to their right where a tall, dark blond man stood with a slender older woman. "That is the Duchess of Ravenhurst, is it not?" Claudia recognized her immediately. "But who is the gentleman?"

Helen linked her arm with Claudia's, and together they walked toward the couple. "He, my dear, could be the man of your dreams!" she whispered dramatically.

Claudia rolled her eyes at that statement but allowed Helen to move them closer. "Helen, I believe you have read one too many romance novels. I couldn't possibly determine whether a man is right for me by just one loo. . . ." Her words drifted to a close as she was finally able to see his face and broad shoulders clearly.

He was dressed in a dark brown riding jacket, beige breeches, and shiny black Hessians. "Oh! He's quite handsome, is he not?" she said breathlessly. Claudia was so engrossed in her perusal of him that she was not aware she had come to a complete stop.

Helen smiled at Claudia and tugged on her arm again. "You can be assured he will soon be the most sought-after gentleman in all of England."

"But who is he? Why have I not met him before?"

"He is Cameron Montbatten, the Earl of Kinclary and heir to the Duke of Ravenhurst," Helen informed her. "And you have not met him for he has been away at school and abroad. I heard from Christina that he's only just returned this week."

Christina was married to the Earl of Kenswick and a friend to Claudia and Helen. The two of them slowed as they neared the bridge. Claudia scrambled to remember if she had been introduced to the duchess and was glad to recall she had. If she had not, then it would be improper to approach her directly.

But the greeting did not go as she had imagined. The moment Claudia stepped forward to make her presence known to them, Lord Kinclary turned to speak with another gentleman. And before Claudia could wonder at his rather abrupt behavior, Lady Ravenhurst spoke up. "Lady Claudia. How nice to see you on this lovely morning."

It became noticeable at once that the older woman had left Helen out of the greeting. "I am doing quite well, your grace," she returned. She reasoned that she was ignoring Helen because they had not been properly introduced. "And may I present my friend, the Lady Northingshire?"

Claudia could not believe it when the duchess cut her sharp gaze to Helen and sneered. "My dear," she said, bringing her gaze back to Claudia, "you should be careful in choosing your friends. You don't want your position amongst the ton damaged beyond repair, do you?"

Claudia gasped then glanced at Helen and saw the hurt

brimming in her vivid blue eyes. "I beg your pardon," she said to the older woman, only to have Helen put her hand on her arm, stopping her words.

"Claudia, I believe I see my husband waiting for me. You'll excuse me, won't you?" she whispered then hurried away, her shoulders slumped in defeat.

Though Claudia had spent two years in England being tutored, instructed, and sometimes prodded on the proper way a lady should comport herself in every situation, she was about to undo it all. She opened her mouth to tell the older woman exactly how she felt when the son suddenly turned back to her and smiled.

The earl was so handsome that it fairly took her breath away to receive his full attention. She had to give herself a mental shake and remember how he'd just ignored her dear friend.

The cad!

"You are not about to leave, are you? Mother, please introduce me to this lovely creature before she escapes," his deep voice urged, his eyes dancing playfully.

She caught her breath again as his moss-green gaze swept over her face. She reasoned it might be best to leave quickly and say nothing at all before this man, who was obviously a practiced charmer where ladies were concerned, made her forget she was upset with him.

"This is Lady Claudia, the future Marchioness of Moreland. An inherited title, I might add," Lady Ravenhurst said. "I was about to ask her to join us for tea sometime. And, my lady," she said, turning to Claudia, "this is my son, Lord Kinclary."

Claudia was already backing away from him even as he bowed to her. "I'm afraid. . .I must go," she stammered. Before he could give her another one of his lethal looks, she turned and dashed away in the direction Helen had gone.

&

In all of his twenty-seven years Cameron could not remember

meeting any woman who affected him as Lady Claudia just had. She barely spoke to him, and yet he knew he must see her again.

"Well, I must say, she reacted very rudely to you, Cam. But what can you expect from those barbaric colonists?" Cameron's mother tugged at her pristine white gloves.

Cameron's brow rose with interest as he gazed at the lady's retreating figure. "Mother, it's been many years since they've been referred to as 'colonists,' and I can only guess her urgency to leave our presence must have been because you said something to insult her," he stated dryly. His mother, Margaret Montbatten, had the ridiculous notion that everyone valued and even begged for her opinion.

Lady Ravenhurst sniffed. "Nonsense! I only told her she should keep better company."

Cameron ran his hand through his hair and groaned aloud. "Mother, the Duke of Northingshire is one of my oldest friends, and now you are telling me you just offended his wife?" He shook his head, wondering how he could repair the damage. "Lady Northingshire is a lovely girl and apparently a good friend of Lady Claudia's—in whom, I might add, I am very interested."

His mother seemed indifferent to his chastisement and ignored his last comment. "Lady Northingshire is a farmer's daughter and better suited to a barnyard than a ballroom. Marrying a duke does not make one a duchess!"

Cameron looked at his mother, who was still pretty for her age, and wondered if she were going senile. "Yes, it does, Mother."

Lady Ravenhurst narrowed her eyes at her son. "Do not be smart with me, young man. I know she is a duchess. I was simply making a point." Then her eyes widened suddenly. "What do you mean you are interested in Lady Claudia? Have you met her before?"

Cameron sighed and tried not to fathom his mother's way of thinking. "I met her only today, but I know she is someone I should like to see more."

"Hmm." Lady Ravenhurst tapped her gloved finger on her cheek. "She is a bit of a rustic, but I have it on good faith that she is a favorite of the prince regent."

Cameron shook his head and took his mother's arm. Together they walked forward. "I care nothing of what the ton thinks," he said firmly. "Now tell me how an American girl becomes the heir to a title."

Cameron listened to his mother tell him about the Marquis of Moreland and how he'd named Claudia his heir. She ended by saying, "She clearly needs tutoring in the ways of a lady, but she has excellent bloodlines despite her mother and would make you a fine countess and future duchess."

"Mother, we are talking about a lady not a horse!" Cameron exclaimed with exasperation, then softened his tone. "You must know what it is like to want to find the perfect mate for your life—someone to share your dreams with and a life full of meaning and purpose. Someone God has chosen for you." He'd taken his mother's hands in his.

His mother stared at him. "What nonsense! Marriage is a merger of two good families who produce superior children, particularly a male, to carry on the line. This cycle has been repeated for centuries. It's the way of things, you know." She pulled her hands away from him, tugged again at her gloves, smoothed her skirts, then took his arm. "Now let's put this romantic foolishness aside and start planning your marriage to the future Marchioness of Moreland."

Cameron sighed and continued to walk alongside his mother. He knew his parents were fond of each other but married because it had been arranged and nothing more. Cameron wanted more. In his travels he'd become friends with a missionary who had such a zeal for God and a strong calling to share God's love to others. It made Cameron ashamed of the selfish life of privilege he'd taken for granted and prodded him to search for a better way to live—one that would please God.

He had found a way to do that, but he felt certain no lady from his world would understand or even want to be a part of it. It would take a special woman, with a similar aspiration, to be his wife.

He was in the midst of wondering about Lady Claudia when a young woman appeared at his other side.

"Ah, Aurora," his mother said. "Your aunt Martin is here with you?"

Lady Aurora Wyndham linked her arm with Cameron's and nodded to his mother. "Good morning, your grace. Yes, she is over there speaking with Lady Exeter."

When Cameron's mother had left to speak with Aurora's aunt, Aurora tugged on his arm and led him behind a large tree.

Cameron had known Aurora since childhood and was fond of her, but he was in no mood to deal with her theatrics. "Aurora, what—," he began impatiently.

"Cam, I've just come from speaking with Father, and I fear I have some terrible news!" She held a white lace handkerchief to her cheek.

Cameron stopped short of rolling his eyes at her. Aurora tended to make even the slightest problem a major ordeal. "What is it, Aurora?"

"He has demanded I become engaged in one month, or he'll make me marry Lord Carmichael. The man is old and toothless and has already been through four wives!" She dabbed at her eyes, though Cameron was sure he saw no tears. "I could not bear to marry such an ogre, Cam. You must help me."

Cameron let out a sigh. "Aurora, you have had countless offers for your hand; yet you have chosen to turn them all down. Your father is just trying to force you to make a decision.

I doubt he will follow through on his threat."

But Aurora would not be calmed. She began to pace in front of him, twisting the handkerchief. "You did not see his face, Cameron. He was serious—of *that* I have no doubt." She stopped and faced him with pleading eyes. "Will you help me?"

As Cameron stared down into Aurora's face, he had no doubt that her luminous gaze, pouty lips, and soft, whispery voice had worked their wiles on many a man. They did not, however, do anything for him except irritate him. "If you are asking me to help you make a match before your father carries out his threat, then I'll do what I can," he said finally.

A smile curved her lips as she reached out to take his arm. "I knew I could count on you, Cam," she cooed and continued to chatter on about something else, but Cameron had stopped listening.

He was already thinking about when and where he might see the lovely Lady Claudia once more.

two

"I beg you to reconsider this ridiculous plan, Claudia," Helen pleaded. She was helping her fasten the buttons on Claudia's shimmering, pale-green gown of silk and beaded taffeta. Her brunette hair was twisted artfully in a turban of the same color as her gown while a few strands framed her face.

Claudia examined her appearance. She knew she was dressed as well as anyone at the ball would be, but she still felt as if she would never fit in.

"It must be done, Helen! The Montbattens, especially Lord Kinclary, think themselves far above almost everyone. Christina told me he had even tried to fight a duel with his sister's husband while they were engaged." She adjusted the emerald and diamond necklace at her throat. Lord Kinclary's sister Katherine was now married to Lord Thomas Thornton, brother to the Earl of Kenswick and brother-in-law to their dear friend Christina. "Someone has to stand up to him and say it is enough."

Helen sighed audibly as she grabbed the gloves from Claudia's dressing table and handed them to her. "As much as you adore the Thornton brothers and their wives, you are only doing this for my sake, and I wish you would not. North might find out, and he will make an even bigger scene over their snubbing me."

Claudia pulled on the last glove then took Helen's hands into her own. "Helen, of course I am doing this for you. But you do not have to worry about your husband finding out, for I shall be most circumspect in my dealings with him."

Helen sighed. "But do you have to do this at a ball—*his*

mother's ball? I do not care that they didn't include me on the invitation. I'm most sure it was just an oversight."

Claudia squeezed Helen's hands and then let them go so she could slip into her hooded cloak. "Of course Lady Montbatten meant it, and I would not doubt that her son had something to do with it also." She tied the cape over her shoulders and faced her friend again. "Helen, we are each entitled to be respected no matter who we are or what station of life we are born to. We are all created equal and have God-given rights which are. . .uh. . .life. . .and liberty and"—she thought a moment then snapped her fingers—"the pursuit of happiness. It's our constitutional right!" She threw her arms up, making her cape rise like wings on either side of her.

Helen looked at her strangely, then burst into laughter. "But we're in England."

Claudia clamped her hand over her mouth and joined her friend's laughter. "Oh, dear. We Americans can wax patriotic at the oddest times, I'm afraid."

Helen smiled, though Claudia could see she was still trying to get hold of her giggles. "Just please don't do that at the ball," she admonished, waggling her finger at her. "I can imagine you marching into the Montbattens' ballroom, waving your American flag, and dumping tea into their fountains in protest."

Claudia giggled and straightened her cape, which had become askew. "Perhaps I'll don the beaded leather dress one of my Choctaw friends made for me before I left and mark my face with war paint."

Helen walked to Claudia's bed then returned with a satin purse. "As fun as that would be to witness, I'm afraid you'll have to leave your war paint at home and face the wolves with only your wits to guard you." She handed her the purse and added, "Unless I can talk you into going to my house. I do have a brand new novel we can read to each other."

Claudia raised her brow and narrowed her gaze at her friend. "I just thought of something. You never told me how your husband reacted when he saw the invitation made out only to him."

Helen looked at the floor. "Well. . .I didn't exactly show him the invitation." She started picking at imaginary lint on her cream-colored skirt. "I told him it had arrived and suggested we miss this one and attend the Beckingham ball tomorrow night." She looked up and met Claudia's gaze. "But shouldn't we leave this matter in God's hands? He will deal with the Montbattens as they deserve."

"Of course, but don't you think God enlists our help on occasion to make people aware of their bad manners?" She smiled at her friend. "God does not mean for you to endure such disrespect—you are His child. You are also the Duchess of Northingshire, and nothing they do or say will change that fact. But tonight perhaps I can make one man understand his actions are petty and mean. I only pray he has some decent, God-fearing part inside him that can be reasoned with."

She turned toward the mirror one last time, and after taking a deep breath squared her shoulders. "Well, I'm ready. You'll say a prayer for me tonight?"

Helen looked at her in the mirror and nodded her head slowly. "I shall be praying all night, for I fear you'll need it."

"I will come and visit you on the morrow and tell you about it," Claudia said to Helen as they walked out of the room to go to their respective carriages. "I'm sure I'll have good news about how the earl saw the error of his ways and will bring you his apology." She prayed her statement would prove true.

Claudia's great-aunt Julia, who acted as her chaperone, was in the carriage and had fallen asleep as usual. Claudia would wake her up when they arrived, and after greeting the key members of her circle her aunt would find a nice comfortable chair and fall asleep again. Claudia smiled to herself and looked out the window as the carriage began to move. At least she didn't have to worry about her aunt reporting back to her grandfather that she had sought the audience of one Earl of Kinclary.

Since the Montbattens' London home was only two blocks from her grandfather's, she and her aunt were soon standing at the grand entrance to the ballroom, and their names were being announced.

She observed a few nods of greeting and curious looks as they entered, especially from some of the young men who'd been vying for her attention lately; but mostly she entered unnoticed since the party was in full swing. Aunt Julia went her way, and Claudia walked down the few steps onto the ballroom floor, casually glancing about in hopes of spotting Lord Kinclary.

"Ah, Lady Claudia!" She looked to her right and saw Lady Ravenhurst hurrying over to her. "I had almost given up on your gracing us with your presence this evening," the older woman said in a sugary voice that surprised Claudia. Since their last meeting at the park had been such an unpleasant one, she had not expected Lady Ravenhurst to be so nice to her. "Cameron was just telling me he hoped you would save him a dance."

Claudia wondered why. Then suddenly the woman's agreeable attitude made sense. Lady Ravenhurst must have high hopes for her son and Claudia. "I don't really dance—"

"Oh, nonsense!" Lady Ravenhurst scanned the room. "Oh, there he is—standing by the painting of the Battle of Waterloo. We just added it to our collection, so I'm sure Cameron would love to show it to you."

Claudia looked about the room and noticed that all the paintings depicted different battles. Very strange décor for a ballroom, she thought. She wondered how she'd figure out which one was of Waterloo. "Um. . .I don't know—"

"Hurry along, dear, before another young lady monopolizes his time. We wouldn't want that, would we?" she whispered knowingly, as if the two of them shared a secret.

"I beg your par—," she started to say, but Lady Ravenhurst had already turned and walked away. Claudia stared after her, trying to make sense of the one-sided conversation she'd just been a part of. Lady Ravenhurst was the rudest and quite possibly the strangest woman she'd ever met. She almost felt sorry for Lord Kinclary.

Almost.

She turned to the room at large then, and it was as if Moses himself had raised his staff because the crowd parted slightly, giving her a clear path to where the handsome earl stood.

And he was indeed handsome, she thought, walking toward him. His dark blond hair seemed as untamed as it had been in the park, falling over his forehead and curling about his neck in a style longer than was fashionable. His dark grey coat and breeches fit him expertly, giving him an air of importance.

It was not unlike watching the stance of an Indian warrior, which she'd encountered many times in Louisiana. In fact she could almost imagine him in buckskins, wearing the feathers of a chief with his long hair flowing in the wind.

"Would you like a glass of punch, my lady?" a server asked, stepping in front of her and waking her from her odd musings. Claudia shook her head, dismissing the servant. She took a deep breath and cleared her head of her fanciful thoughts.

How could she admire a man who was so obviously a snob and a cad?

I couldn't, of course, she assured herself as she started to walk again, only to find the object of her thoughts was no longer standing by the painting.

Still feeling a bit flustered, she surveyed the room and finally found him by the painting of another battle, speaking to a pretty woman in a light pink dress.

Claudia felt a pang of something that reminded her of jealousy when she saw the way the earl was smiling at the woman. But after reasoning with herself that she couldn't feel jealousy when she didn't even *like* the man, she headed in his direction again.

She was almost there when he looked up and met Claudia's gaze. On seeing her, his eyes lit up, and his lips curved into a smile.

Suddenly she realized she was smiling back at him like a lovesick buffoon.

"Lady Claudia," he said in his low soft voice, "I had hoped you would come."

Claudia told herself over and over that she was here for Helen's sake. She would not be charmed by this rogue, even though his words seemed to pour over her like honey and run straight to her heart.

"Lord Kinclary," she said coolly, "I had wanted to see you also."

She didn't think it was possible, but his green eyes seemed to brighten even more, and Claudia knew her words had been misinterpreted.

And not just by the earl. "Ahem!" The young woman beside him threw her a speculative look before gazing back up at Lord Kinclary. "Cameron, won't you introduce us?" The woman nearly purred, and Claudia wondered if the high, syrupy tone was her natural voice or one she used only around men.

Claudia did not miss the familiar use of his Christian name either. The young woman was crafty.

It seemed almost a chore for Cameron to draw his gaze from Claudia to peer down at the woman demanding his attention. "Hmm? Ah. . .yes," he murmured. "Aurora, this is Lady Claudia, granddaughter of the Marquis of Moreland. Lady Claudia, this is Lady Aurora, daughter of Lord Donald Wyndham."

The ladies bobbed a polite curtsy to one another, though Aurora accompanied hers with a glare.

Claudia didn't know if it was the effect Lord Kinclary had on her or the dislike radiating from the other woman, but she wanted to do what she came to do and go home. "Lord Kinclary, I need to have a word with you, if you don't mind."

Cameron raised his brow at her. "Of course you may."

Claudia noticed Lady Aurora hadn't taken the hint, for she stood stock-still, as though she should be privy to the conversation. She was about to ask her bluntly to leave, but Lord Kinclary did it for her.

"You'll excuse us, won't you, Aurora?"

Aurora smiled, though it didn't reach her dark eyes. "Of course. I'll be right back," she said, leaving Claudia to wonder about what sort of relationship she and the earl shared.

"I am all yours, Lady Claudia," he said in a low voice. He took her gloved hand and brought it to his lips. Her head snapped up to meet his gaze, and she was stunned by the admiration gleaming there. "I have been thinking about you these last three days since we met."

For some reason his words irritated Claudia. Perhaps they were too practiced, or he seemed so confident the attraction was mutual. Whatever it was, it made her more determined to carry out the plan.

She jerked her hand away before he could kiss it and held it to her chest as though she'd been stung. "Lord Kinclary! Please!"

Surprised, but not thwarted, he responded, "Please call me Cameron, and forgive me if I've acted too forwardly. But when you said you had come to see me—"

She gasped. "Do you believe I sought you out because I've been pining away for you for three days? What sort of woman do you take me for, *Lord Kinclary*?" She refused to address him familiarly.

He was silent as he scanned her face. "I apologize for the offense, my lady," he said calmly. "Please tell me why you've come."

Claudia was surprised he didn't seem put out by her rejection of his advances. If he had been thinking about her for the last three days, shouldn't he be more upset that she apparently hadn't been doing the same?

She drew in a breath and made herself stop trying to figure out the man. "A friend of mine has been truly offended by your actions and by those of your mother. I feel I must speak out in her defense. I don't understand the need for higher classes to snub those of lower birth, especially when this person is such a lovely, sweet girl who would never return such an offense. I mean—"

"Excuse me, my lady, but I have no idea of whom you speak," he said, interrupting her.

Claudia had expected him to remember the situation. Was he such a blackguard that he could dismiss someone without so much as an afterthought? "I, *sir*, am speaking of the Duchess of Northingshire, the lady you ignored whilst your mother lashed insults upon her. It is insufferable that you could be so coldhearted as to deliberately hurt someone of such a gentle and loving character."

"Lady Claudia!" he exclaimed in a whisper. "You have misjudged me, and as far as my mother is concerned I cannot be held accountable for what she might have said or done."

Claudia shook her head. "But—"

"Wait." he whispered again as he glanced about the room. She followed his gaze and saw that people were beginning to stare at them. "This is not the place to discuss this. If you will wait for me on the terrace, I will follow directly."

She was about to say no but thought better of it. She was curious as to what he had to say, but she did not want gossip to be started about the two of them. She nodded and turned then walked out into the cool night air.

❧

As Cameron watched Lady Claudia walk away, he tried to

think why she considered him to be such a malicious person. Of course she hadn't told him what his mother had said to the duchess. Whatever had transpired, it must have been rude and cutting. He had to admire the lady, though, for defending a friend so loyally even though she herself could risk being hurt socially for it.

Cameron was more intrigued than ever by the beautiful American, and he hoped he could clear up the matter so he could begin calling on her.

After several minutes he decided enough time had passed. He stepped toward the glass doors leading to the terrace. Suddenly Aurora stood in his path.

She began speaking to him, but he was only half listening when he spotted Claudia through the windows, standing by the stone railing.

Waiting for him. Cameron smiled at those words and wondered what it would be like for her to be waiting for him at home as his wife. He scarcely knew her, but the thought of pursuing a relationship with Lady Claudia felt fitting somehow.

". . .marry me."

Aurora's words sounded like a gun firing in his ears. "What did you say?" he demanded, wishing he'd paid more attention. Aurora had a way of talking him into things without his being aware he'd agreed.

Aurora sighed then curled her lips in a pout. "I'm telling you my life is in a shambles, and you are not even listening," she said with a sniff.

His patience was already thin. "Aurora, I meant, what were you saying about someone marrying you?"

She moistened her lips and smiled weakly at him. "I said I'm having trouble finding someone to marry me. And since you are my oldest and dearest friend I am asking you to save me from the fate my father has laid out for me."

Cameron was appalled at the thought of having to marry

Aurora. She was like a sister to him—and a sometimes annoying sister at that. "Aurora, you still have more than three weeks to find a husband. And I promise to do everything within my power to help you find one," he assured her.

She shook her head, and her eyes filled with tears. It was because she was frightened about marrying Lord Carmichael, wasn't it? Surely she felt about him as he did her—like a sibling?

"But if I can't, Cameron, you must save me," she cried softly as she reached out to clutch his arm. "Please promise me you'll marry me if I cannot find anyone else."

His throat tightened in panic as he stared down at Aurora. He didn't want her to have to marry a man who'd had his share of wives; neither did he desire to sacrifice himself.

He looked away from her and let his gaze drift to the terrace.

Claudia was no longer there.

Alarmed, he tried to step around Aurora, but she stopped him. "You didn't answer me, Cameron. Will you promise me?"

He knew she would not leave him alone until he agreed. He only prayed he could find her a husband in time. "Yes, I promise," he said hurriedly. "Now if you'll excuse me—"

He dashed outside without waiting for a response then walked to the far right of the terrace but discovered it was empty. He looked at the other end and saw a gate. He felt certain she must be walking in the garden, but when he reached the gate he found it locked.

Cameron peered over the railing and down at the ground several feet below him. With no other doors to go through and no way to get to the garden, he couldn't figure out where she had gone.

And then he spotted a small piece of torn fabric wedged into the iron leaves on the top of the gate.

It was green silk.

three

Claudia squeezed through the hedge and made her way to the street. What fun to climb over the gate and run through the Montbatten garden! It had helped alleviate some of her annoyance at watching Lord Kinclary—*Cameron*—flirting with Lady Aurora while he was supposed to be finishing his conversation with her.

The scoundrel!

Claudia looked back at the large townhouse and remembered her aunt was still inside. She shivered from the cold night air—and realized she had left her cape in there also. She debated whether or not she should go back inside and retrieve them both but knew she did not want to see the earl again. She was so irritated at him that she might say or do something irreparable.

So she was committing a social *faux pas* by walking alone and would need a really clever explanation of why she left the ball without her aunt. Claudia felt it was worth it. Hugging her arms around her, she started the short walk to her grandfather's home.

Claudia had just rounded the corner and started down a particularly dark street when she was seized from behind. She opened her mouth to scream, but a rough hand clamped hard over it. Another hand wrapped around her waist and pulled her back against the offender's chest.

Fear and panic set in, but she kept herself still until her mind could think rationally. Maybe someone was playing a trick on her as her Choctaw friend, Sam, had done many times back in Louisiana. But the moment she smelled his foul breath at her cheek and the coarse wool scraping her arm, she knew this man was no friend.

" 'Ello, princess. Wot do we 'ave 'ere?" His gravelly voice grated in her ear, while his hand clutched at the jewels around her neck. Claudia thought she could twist free, but then she felt the cool touch of metal at her throat and realized he was holding a knife. "Set'le down, princess. All I want is ye pretty baubles. Me wife will look right fine wi' them lovelies 'round 'er neck."

Claudia shivered not from the night air but from sheer terror, her cries muffled by the man's hand. She felt the sting of the knife blade scraping her skin as he lifted the necklace.

Her arms and hands still unbound, Claudia knew she had to get away or he would no doubt kill her. She raised her foot and stomped down as hard as she could with the heel of her boot into the soft leather of his boot. The man yelled and loosened his hold on her, enough for her to push the knife away from her throat and grab his other hand which she bit.

The man swore with words she'd never heard. She broke away from him and started to run. But he caught her and pressed the knife even harder against her throat while the other held her arms tight behind her. "Now yuv done it," he growled. "I'll make ye pay for that."

Claudia's breath came in short gasps. "Ple–please, sir," she cried. "You can have the jewels. Just please let me—"

Suddenly he let go of her, the knife slicing through her gown and shoulder with one painful swipe. Shocked, she grabbed at her shoulder and turned slowly to find Cameron Montbatten slapping the knife away from the man then knocking him to the ground with one solid punch.

The man, so menacing and frightening before, was lying prostrate on the ground with his hands out, begging Cameron to let him go. Cameron made a growling noise, which seemed so out of character for his usual calm and charming self. He stooped over and pulled the man off the ground then twisted his arm behind his back.

Claudia stood frozen watching the scene before her, then saw him call to his waiting carriage for one of his footmen to tie up the man and take him to the police.

Only when Cameron had released the man to his servant did he finally turn to her. Her heart melted when she saw his face so filled with concern.

"Are you all right?" he asked softly. He walked over to her and reached out his hand to caress her cheek.

Claudia swallowed hard and leaned toward him, wondering if he would offer a comforting embrace. "I believe he only wounded my shoulder," she answered, though in truth she no longer felt the pain. Just being near him seemed to make everything. . .better.

His hand left her cheek, and he inspected the wound on her arm. "You're bleeding!"

Now he'll probably take me in his arms. She started to reach toward him.

"Are you out of your mind?" he roared, and her waiting arms fell back to her side. Her confused gaze flew to his, and she was surprised by the angry scowl on his handsome face. "Every young woman in England knows better than to walk the streets of London alone at night. I should think you'd take better care of yourself than to do something this foolish."

Claudia gaped at him then cried, "You're angry with me? I am accosted and nearly killed, and, instead of comforting me as a gentleman should, you yell at me as if it's all *my* fault?"

Cameron shook his head then ran his hand through his hair. "That is precisely what it is—your fault." He threw his hands in the air. "You should have stayed on the terrace and waited for me. Instead you scampered over the gate like a wild Indian, tearing your dress and risking your reputation as well as your life. Is this what they taught you in your country?"

"Of all the nerve!" Claudia gasped. "I'll have you know, I'd rather be an Indian *and* an American any day than a snobbish, arrogant, prideful—*dandy*—like you." And with that she twirled about and started walking again.

She didn't get very far because he took her arm in a gentle grip and turned her back around. "Where do you think you're going?"

"Home, if you don't mind." She stared at his hand on her arm.

He shook his head. "Oh, no, you're not. We're going to my home and let my valet clean your wound. If you go to your grandfather's looking like this, he'll lock you up for the rest of the season."

He must know my grandfather, for that's exactly what he would do. She saw no other recourse. "All right. But if you start yelling at me again, I'll—well, I'll"—she searched for the right words—"I'll do something. You can be assured of it!" she finally finished. She knew he was hardly listening as he guided her to his large, black carriage.

Once they were inside, she was surprised when he sat beside her on the cramped padded seat instead of across from her. It was an obvious attempt for him to show her he was in charge and that she must be looked after like a child.

"How is your arm? Can you tell if it's still bleeding?" he asked quietly.

She sensed his concern but no longer wanted or needed it. "What? Are you afraid I might bleed all over your fine velvet?"

Her barb only elicited a chuckle from him. "There is that—and if you bleed to death your grandfather might never believe I'm completely innocent in this whole affair."

Claudia made a huffing sound, removed her bloodstained glove, and put her hand to her shoulder. The pain was back, and though it was a bit sticky she could tell it was no longer bleeding badly. "I suppose it's all right," she told him with a deliberately weak voice. There was no reason to make him feel better after the way he had talked to her.

It worked. "I'm going to move to your other side so I can examine it." He got up, and she slid over; but the bumpiness of the carriage made it difficult for him to sit down carefully. He knocked her shoulder on his way down.

"Oww! Now it really hurts!" She wished she had told him the truth in the first place. *Serves me right.*

"I am truly sorry," Cameron told her, cupping her shoulder with his hands and carefully laying aside the torn pieces of her gown.

"It's dark, Cameron. How will you tell if it's all right or not?" Too late, Claudia realized she'd used his Christian name. She only hoped he hadn't.

But he had.

"There is a little light from the moon. Now keep still and say my name one more time."

She could almost hear the smile in his voice. She wished she would mind her tongue better. "That was a mistake."

He took out his handkerchief, lay it over the wound, and tied it under her armpit. "If you say it, I promise not to yell at you anymore," he whispered near her ear, causing chills to race down her arms.

She glanced at him. "I don't even like you," she declared, though she knew it wasn't true. "And I doubt you'll have an opportunity to yell at me again since we shall never see one another after this night." She tilted her chin up and looked away.

"Oh, come now. Of course you like me. I can tell," he assured her, leaning closer.

"You are extremely overconfident and arrogant—"

"Yes, you've said that."

"*And* I could never like someone with those annoying qualities," she finished despite his interruption.

"You can prove it by saying my name."

She glanced at him again and could barely make out his features in the darkness. She had enough light, though, to see his teasing, self-assured smile.

Very irritating.

"This is ridiculous. Saying your name will prove nothing."

"No, no. When a lady speaks a man's name while looking him in the eyes, he can tell how she truly feels about him."

Claudia didn't believe a word of what he was saying but decided to play along. With the sternest glare she could muster and as little emotion as possible she started to say his name.

"Camer—"

Suddenly his lips descended upon hers. She was so surprised she did nothing but let him kiss her. And when the shock began to dissipate she found she actually *liked* his kissing her.

In fact Claudia was about to kiss him back when Cameron broke the kiss as abruptly as he had started it.

ఈ

Cameron could not comprehend what caused him to kiss her. Perhaps it was her beautiful face glowing so prettily in the moonlight, or perhaps he had felt like her conquering hero. Whatever it was, he had acted in a way he never had before.

He tried to catch his breath and sort out his feelings on the matter, but a resounding slap on his cheek knocked him sideways.

"Ow! I beg your—"

"How dare you, you—you—cad!" she sputtered as any proper young miss had a right to. "What do you take me for? I am a lady, and we are not betrothed."

"Would you like to be?" Cameron asked without thinking.

With a cry of frustration she leaped from her seat to sit across from him. "No, I would not like to be, you—scoundrel!"

Cameron couldn't help himself. He laughed. "Do young ladies sit around all day thinking of names to call gentlemen when they are vexed with them?"

Claudia shook her finger at him. "Do not change the subject. I want an apology and a promise you will never kiss me again!"

Cameron stared at her from across the carriage and grinned. "Well, I do apologize for kissing you. Even though I enjoyed it enormously"—Claudia gasped, but he continued—"it was not the right time and place for it to happen. But I cannot promise I will *not* kiss you again."

"Why not?" she cried.

Cameron slid over to her side of the carriage and made her move to accommodate him. "Because I plan to do it again someday."

He could tell she was scrambling to find another name to call him but was saved when the carriage finally stopped.

Cameron climbed out first and tried to help her from the carriage, but she refused his hand and managed to get down herself. He had the urge to laugh again at her stubbornness but kept himself under control. He'd been called enough outrageous names tonight anyway.

It took only a moment for his butler, George, to answer the door and let them inside. George eyed Claudia as Cameron had known he would; he realized he had to get her into his study before any of the other servants saw and recognized her. Servants were notorious gossips and could easily ruin her reputation for being in a single man's home alone.

"George, this young woman was attacked after she exited the ball tonight. Do you think you can call for Brooks and have him bring his medical kit down here?" Brooks was his valet and could help with minor medical emergencies.

The older man's demeanor changed when he saw the blood and the makeshift bandage on Claudia's shoulder. "Right away, my lord."

He looked at Claudia's face then, and their gazes met. Cameron watched them stare at one another for a moment.

Then George turned and walked up the large staircase to Cameron's rooms.

Cameron looked at Claudia and saw she was still following his butler with her gaze. "Is something amiss? Do you know George?"

She regarded him blankly then shook her head. "No, I. . ." Her words drifted off. "I don't think I know him, but he did seem familiar to me." She smiled and shrugged. "Perhaps the loss of blood has made me a bit dopey."

Cameron smiled and motioned toward a large door off the foyer. "Let's go in my study so we can tend to your wound."

As soon as he had made her comfortable, his valet came in. Brooks checked the wound but assured them it wasn't deep and needed no stitches. He smeared some sort of medicine on it and bandaged it up.

After he left the room Cameron offered her a cup of tea George had brought in for her to drink before he took her home.

"Now that we are calm and thinking rationally," Cameron began as she sipped the hot brew, "perhaps you can tell me why you dashed off before I could get out to the terrace."

Claudia sighed and set the cup in its saucer. "I saw you speaking to Lady Aurora through the window and thought you'd forgotten about me." She quickly picked up the cup and took another sip of tea as if to hide her embarrassment for confessing such a thing.

Cameron smiled and noted the soft pink of her cheeks. "I don't believe I could ever forget you, Claudia," he told her gently. "Why did you not simply go back into the ballroom?"

She shrugged. "I feel so out of place at those gatherings. I have to watch everything I say or do, and even if I am on my best behavior, someone finds fault with me. I suppose I just felt like—being free."

"North has told me of the time he spent in Louisiana

getting to know your family. It's sounds very different from England." He hoped she would tell him about herself. He was rewarded by the misty smile that curved her lips.

"It is very different. There were rules, of course, and even society gatherings, but things were more relaxed. My sister and I would climb trees, row our pirogues down the bayou, and play with the Choctaw Indian children." She glanced at him and grinned. "I suppose I must sound very uncivilized to you."

"Actually it sounds delightful." He could hardly believe this warm, wonderful woman who was sharing her childhood with him was the same one showering him with insults an hour ago. But then he liked both her spunk and her sweetness. She was so unlike any woman he'd ever met, and he found he had a hunger to know more. "My childhood was nothing but tutors, boarding school, and then university. I suppose that's why I traveled around the Continent for a year, to have a change of scenery and know the world I'd been learning about."

He took her empty teacup and saucer and set it on the table. "When you are the heir to a dukedom you spend your whole life getting ready for it. It can make for a very lonely existence."

"I've only had two years to prepare for my title, and it scares me I'll be handed too much responsibility when my grandfather passes on. At least you'll be more prepared."

He gazed at her a moment. "Perhaps your husband can assist you."

"Not you, too!" She waved her hand as if to ward off his words. "This is all I hear from Grandfather night and day. I must find a husband before I am too old and no one will want me. It puts a lot of pressure on a lady to hear that, especially since I have not met anyone I am remotely attracted to."

This was not what Cameron hoped to hear. "Surely you've met someone."

She stood and gazed about his room. "No. No one." She

picked up an animal figurine from his desk and studied it. "Is that what life is all about? Finding someone to marry?" She turned to face him. "Don't you want to do something with your life besides attend balls and be seen riding through Hyde Park? I've always thought God wanted me to do something special, something to help someone."

Cameron wanted to continue the discussion about her earlier comments concerning marriage but found himself intrigued by her passionate admission. "Yes, I have felt that way. I, too, desire to follow the path God has laid out for me. I believe it's in every man who is a Christian to want to do something for the Father's kingdom."

Claudia looked at him, her eyes wide. "You're saying this because you think it's what I want to hear."

He frowned. "I speak the truth."

She pointed the figurine at him. "Oh, no. I spoke to your mother earlier, and she all but admitted she wants us to make a match."

He shook his head. He wondered what his mother had said to her. "What would be wrong with that?" he asked carefully.

"Didn't you hear me earlier? I don't like you. You insulted my friend then left me on the terrace to freeze to death while flirting with that little brunette."

"I didn't intentionally insult your friend, and I wasn't flirting with anyone. I saved your life tonight! Doesn't it prove to you I'm a good person?"

"Yes, but then you yelled at me instead of comforting me. What sort of gentleman does that?"

Cameron ran his hands through his hair and wondered how the conversation had gone so wrong. "What you did was insane! I felt it my duty to point out to you the error of your ways."

"Well, you can tell your mother that if and when I find a man I want to marry he will be gentle and kind and. . .know how a woman wants to be treated after she's been accosted!"

Cameron shook his head. "I doubt there is a man in all the world who could live up to your lofty standards. And if there is, will he be able to live with your ever-changing moods?"

Claudia gasped, and Cameron regretted his words. How could a woman twist him inside out as this one could? He barely knew her, and he was already torn between wringing her neck and kissing her again.

"I think it's time you took me home," she said stiffly, setting the figurine back on his desk. Without looking at him again, she marched toward the door.

Cameron opened his mouth to apologize but knew it probably would do no good. Instead he grabbed the cloak his butler had brought down for her. Claudia allowed him to put it around her but said nothing else to him on the way to her grandfather's house.

Once they'd arrived, he helped her out of the carriage, despite her efforts to ignore him. "Good night, my lady," he said softly as he walked her to the door.

He thought he would get no response, but apparently good breeding wouldn't allow her to be that rude.

She stopped and said in a crisp tone, "Good-bye."

He smiled then, already looking forward to the next time their paths would cross.

four

Claudia slipped undetected into her grandfather's house and hid the ruined gown until she could dispose of it, then settled down into her soft bed for the night. She longed for sleep to overtake her so she could forget both the man who had attacked her and the man who had saved her.

But the latter was not easily forgotten, so sleep did not come.

Of all the eligible men in London, why did she have to feel such an attraction to the Earl of Kinclary?

"Cameron," she whispered aloud. It seemed natural and right to speak it. It also seemed natural for him to kiss her—and for her to want to kiss him back.

She groaned from the conflicting emotions, then rolled over and hugged her pillow. She reminded herself that the man had yelled at her and hadn't actually explained why he was talking to Aurora so long. Then there were his words to her, echoing her heart's desire to do God's work. Was it a lie, or was he being honest about his feelings?

Claudia was aware she was considered attractive by gentlemen's standards, but she was not insensible to the real reason so many wanted to marry her.

Her grandfather was wealthy and titled. Someday she and her future children would be also.

Claudia frowned as she absently pulled at the lace trim on her silk pillowcase. Cameron was already titled and richer than her grandfather.

Perhaps he truly liked her.

She sighed and flipped back over to stare at the ceiling. She had to remember what he'd said in their last conversation. He believed her to be difficult and moody. If the earl had liked her before, he probably had reconsidered it after her display of bad temper.

Which was just as well, she told herself. After all that had transpired between them, she could never like someone who was so overbearing and arrogant as Lord Kinclary.

But as she drifted off to sleep she knew she did like him.

Very much.

In fact that thought was still ringing in her head when she awoke the next morning. Claudia was so wrapped up in her musings that she didn't notice her grandfather sitting at the breakfast table with her aunt, giving her his most severe glare.

Claudia took a plate and began to fill it from the buffet, scarcely noticing what she was spooning up. Recalling Cameron's kiss, she slipped into her chair and took a bite of her poached egg.

As the taste hit her tongue, she glanced down at her plate in horror and wondered why she would ever choose poached eggs since she hated them.

"Claudia!" her grandfather said sharply.

She looked up at once and saw both her relatives eyeing her strangely.

"Yes? What is it?" She hurriedly swallowed the awful egg and took a sip of milk.

Her grandfather narrowed his eyes, causing his bushy grey brows to join in one line. "I've called your name thrice—yet you do not respond. What is the matter with you this morning?"

"I'm just"—she tried to think of a plausible excuse—"I'm just a bit out of sorts this morning."

He pressed his lips together. A sound came forth much like a growl. "And could this be because you left the ball without your aunt last night—*and* without the aide of my carriage?" His voice grew louder as he neared the end of his sentence.

Claudia cleared her throat. "Well, Grandfather, I was not enjoying myself at the ball, and a"—she nearly choked on the word—"*friend* took me home."

"You were not there to enjoy yourself, girl. You were there to find a husband!" He slammed his fist on the table, causing her aunt to drop her fork with a loud clatter.

"Yes, Grandfather," she murmured. She had heard his thoughts on the subject before.

"And why could you not have taken the time to tell your aunt where you were going?"

Claudia glanced at her aunt who gave her an anxious look while discreetly shaking her head. It was, of course, unnecessary. Claudia would never tell her grandfather that Aunt Julia was asleep within minutes of arriving at the ball.

"Aunt Julia was. . .occupied, Grandfather. I saw no reason to disturb her."

Her grandfather narrowed his eyes again. "You are not playing me for a fool, are you, Claudia? You would not be consorting with someone I would not approve of, would you?"

Claudia sighed. She knew he asked only because of what her own father had done. "No, I am not. I'm not consorting with anyone, so you can rest easy." She took a bite of toast and nearly choked when his hand hit the table again.

"Well, why not? There must be a bevy of young gentlemen who would marry you, girl. Can't you choose one of them?" he bellowed.

Claudia set down her milk, which she'd gulped to wash down the toast. "It's not that easy. I haven't met anyone I could love enough to marry."

"Can't you settle for liking them?" he grumbled, pushing his plate back and folding his arms.

"No, I cannot."

The two of them stared at one another as if they were two duelers on the field ready to spar.

Suddenly Aunt Julia, who rarely said anything to her brother, laughed. "My dear Moreland, she is exactly like you! I doubt you'll win many battles with this one." She stood and walked out of the room.

Claudia's grandfather turned back to her. "She under-estimates me," he stated grimly. "I will see you married. If you cannot find a good Englishman, then we shall travel to Scotland to discover if any of them are to your liking."

Claudia gasped. "What if none of them appeals to me? Will you ship me off to France then?"

Lord Moreland frowned. "Don't be ridiculous. I would rather you marry an American than a Frenchman!" He stood up from the table and shook his finger at her. "Heed my warning, young lady. Find a husband and be quick about it! I'm not getting any younger, you know, and a nobleman likes to know if his line will be carried on." His voice sounded thinner as he spoke, and he punctuated it with a cough.

Once he had turned and was walking out of the room, Claudia rolled her eyes and slumped down in her chair. If threats didn't work, he always played his "old and feeble" routine.

Her thoughts turned to her other grandfather. Was he as gruff as Grandfather Moreland, or was he gentle and loving? She longed to find him and wished someone could give her a clue as to where she might look.

Claudia tapped her fingers on the lace tablecloth until she hit upon an idea. She was to meet with her vicar, Reverend Holloway, this morning to discuss what charities she might be a part of. Perhaps he would know something about her mother's father, George Canterbury.

An hour later she was knocking on the vicar's door. His wife, a petite woman with snow-white hair, greeted her and showed her into the parlor to wait for the vicar.

While she waited, Claudia walked about the room and

examined the titles of his books with interest. She was not an avid reader of fiction but often enjoyed reading about biblical history and commentaries on various religious issues.

She heard a sound from the door, and when she turned, the very tall Reverend Holloway walked in. Just behind him Mrs. Holloway brought in a fresh pot of tea and dainty cups. Claudia could not help but smile when she noticed how much of a height difference there was between them. And, too, she didn't miss the loving smile they shared as he took the tray from her and put it on the table.

Would she ever get the chance to find such a love as these two obviously shared?

Once she had poured the tea, Mrs. Holloway left the room, and Claudia began to explain how she wanted to be a part of one of the church's charities.

"So you want to make a donation?" the vicar asked when she finished.

"Oh, no! I want to take part and do some work myself," she assured him.

Instead of being happy she wanted to help, he hesitated. "Does your. . .uh. . .grandfather know you want to do this?" he asked carefully.

Claudia sighed. Did everyone know how snobbish her grandfather could be? "Well, no. But I want to do this whether he knows or not. I promise that if he finds out, you will shoulder none of the blame."

He hesitated again. "Yes, my lady, but perhaps you don't realize the ways of the ton in this matter. They give their money and throw charity auctions to help the poor, but they don't actually *interact* with the poor. Do you understand?"

Claudia nodded. "Oh, I do know that, Reverend Holloway. And I'm well aware I might be frowned upon, but I feel that God wants me to do this. Do *you* understand?"

The older gentleman smiled at her. "I do. You see, I don't

encounter this type of request every day. Let me check and see what charity could use your help, and I will send a note for you as soon as I know something."

Claudia stood and held out her hand. "Thank you so much, Reverend."

He stood also and shook her hand. "You're most welcome, my lady."

She started to walk out of the room when she remembered what else she wanted to discuss with him. "Oh, by the way, Reverend, I am trying to locate my mother's father, George Canterbury, but have not been able to find out where he might be. Would you happen to know him?"

Reverend Holloway scratched his chin then nodded his head. "I have heard of a Canterbury, but I don't recall where." He paused again then shook his head. "He may be connected with one of the charities along the riverfront. Quite a few feed the poor and administer other helps. Most of them are worthwhile charities, but I cannot refer you to any. The riverfront is a dangerous place for a young woman," he added, but Claudia was too excited by his first statement to worry about his warning.

"Oh, thank you, Reverend. Perhaps the one you are thinking of is a relative who can further my search," she said eagerly. "I'll look forward to hearing from you. Good day," she said quickly then turned and hurried out of the room, not even giving the vicar the chance to say good-bye.

Once she was outside she began walking the short distance to her grandfather's house. Claudia's mind was racing, contemplating how she could get down to the riverfront without being noticed.

Surely the waterfront couldn't be that bad, could it? she wondered. There had to be a way of going down there without being noticed as a gentlewoman and remain safe.

She'd have to rent a hack, of course, for her grandfather would never allow her to take his carriage down there and would lock her up if he thought she was planning to go there herself.

And she most certainly needed a disguise. If only she could think of a way to conceal her identity. . . .

A young boy sitting by the road in ragged clothes caught her attention—and gave her an idea.

❧

That same afternoon on the waterfront Cameron exited the large warehouse and walked to his two-wheeled buggy, whistling a happy tune. Everything he'd been working toward had finally come together.

His shelter for women and their children was birthed upon his arrival back in London. He'd spoken to several clergymen, and they'd told him their biggest problem was women who had lost their husbands or fathers in the war or by some other calamity. They often had no income and no way to support their children. A few churches tried to help them, but the need was so great and their funds often not enough.

So Cameron, along with his butler, George, who acted as the front man for the charity, purchased one of the old warehouses along the wharf and made it habitable. The bulk of his money came from his own pockets, but he'd also managed to procure donations from his closest friends—the ones who would keep his identity private.

Cameron wished he could be more open about his project, but he knew his parents—namely his mother—would oppose it vehemently, declaring it might hurt her standings within the ton. Society might understand his donating money, but they would not accept that he worked at the shelter, overseeing the whole operation.

So, for the time being, he worked discreetly. He let George be the one who spoke to employers about work for the ladies and arranged for food and material to be donated to them from local markets.

Cameron drove along in his buggy and scanned the people who were walking, as he always did, in case he saw women or children who might need the shelter's services. He had come to one of the many public houses along the wharf when he spotted a youth stumbling along the path, apparently lost.

Cameron slowed the buggy. Something about the boy troubled him, and yet he didn't know what. His tattered and soiled clothes seemed to swallow his thin frame, and a dirty cap was pulled down so low it almost covered his eyes. Cameron wondered if he was hungry and decided he must try to get him to the shelter. "Hey! You there! Boy!" he called out, and the youth kept walking.

But then he turned and looked up. Cameron's heart nearly stopped when he recognized those very blue eyes.

five

Frozen with disbelief, Claudia found herself staring into the eyes of Cameron Montbatten. What was he doing in this part of town?

And why was he staring at her so intently?

He pulled back on the reins and climbed down from the buggy. Claudia didn't know if he were coming after her or not, but she wasn't going to wait around to find out.

She pulled her hat even further down on her face and began to run through the sailors, beggars, and general riff-raff that occupied the wharf. *It has been a wasted trip anyway,* she thought as she ducked in between two old wooden buildings. No one had seemed to know anything about a shelter or her grandfather. Most of the people would not even speak to her, thinking her a beggar or thief.

Claudia's breathing was heavy as she peeked around the corner to see if Cameron was still following her. She let out a sigh of relief when she scanned the area and saw no sign of him. With her hand over her chest she turned back and, closing her eyes, slumped against the building.

"What are you doing down here?" a man's voice hissed.

Startled, she opened her eyes to find Cameron standing inches away from her and looking angrier than he ever had, even after she'd been mugged.

Her first thought was to run; but when she started to, he only caught her from behind and brought her back up against his chest. "Do I know you, sir?" she asked in a low, muffled voice.

He let out a sound of frustration then swung her around. While gripping her arm with his hand he cupped her chin and brought it up to meet his fiery gaze. "If I didn't recognize those eyes of yours, that American accent would have given you away," he said, his voice barely controlled. "Now come with me."

Cameron all but dragged Claudia to his buggy and helped her up none-too-gently. She tried to scramble out the other side, but he was much too quick for her. "Claudia, I promise you that my patience is at an end. If you try to get away from me, I'll take you to your grandfather and tell him where I found you."

Cameron snapped the reins with a jerk, and the horses took off, causing Claudia to fall back on the seat. He deftly turned the buggy around in the street and headed back in the opposite direction.

"Where are we going?" she asked, still trying to figure out how this could have happened. Her plan had been so perfect, she thought. She had borrowed clothes from her stable boy and streaked her face with dirt so that not even her own servants had recognized her when she passed them on the street.

She paused from her wonderings when she realized Cameron hadn't answered her. She opened her mouth to ask again but then noticed the muscles tensing in his jaw, so she closed it again and sat still.

The question still burned in her mind—what had he been doing in this wretched part of London?

When the buggy jerked to a stop in front of a large warehouse, Claudia's confusion only increased. Again she found his hand wrapped around her arm like a manacle.

"Come with me, and not a sound do I want to hear from you," he hissed as he pulled her up the steps and into the building.

Claudia wasn't sure what she expected, but twenty or so women and children sitting around a table eating was not it.

What is this place? she wondered, as he pulled her hurriedly through the large room and down the hall to an office.

She'd barely had time to glance at the décor of the office when he started. "In all my days I have not met another woman as troublesome and difficult as you! Nor have I met a highborn lady so bound to ruin her reputation or worse—get herself killed!" He shook his head and stared at her as if she'd suddenly sprouted horns. "What possible reason could you have for risking your life and coming to this part of town? Are you mad? Or do you just not care about your own well-being?"

She bristled at his condescending tone and words. "I'm neither mad nor uncaring. I simply had something I needed to see about down here—that's all," she snapped back and took her hat off to scratch her itching head. "But let me ask you the same question, Lord Kinclary. What are you doing down here in this part of town, and what is this place?" she asked, pointing her finger at him.

"What do you mean that you had something to see about down here? What business could possibly bring you here?" he all but shouted, ignoring her latter question.

"Will you stop yelling at me?" she snapped then turned to sit in one of the chairs in front of his desk. She scratched her head again while examining the dirty cap she'd been wearing. "I hope this didn't give me lice," she murmured.

Cameron walked over and grabbed the cap from her hand and tossed it on his desk. "Lice are the least of your worries!"

She stared up at him, and their gazes held. She found it fascinating to see the emotions that crossed his face. First frustration, then exasperation, then. . .worry? He actually seemed concerned for her.

Her emotions were somewhat raw from their previous encounter, and now being so close to him she tried to fathom why he affected her so much. She was usually so good at dealing with young men and had a way of artfully avoiding their hints of wanting to marry her. Verbal sparring and witty remarks came easily to her, and Claudia often thought she could get out of any trouble as long as she had a voice and a clear mind.

But she was tired of battling with Cameron. She didn't want to dislike him or have him think ill of her.

So she rose slowly from the chair and faced him with her arms folded. "Do you truly think me mad?" she asked softly, nervous as to what his answer might be.

His brows furrowed. Finally he sighed and shook his head. "No, I don't think that at all. It's just that I don't know what to think of you. You seem to do things without any forethought or regard for your own safety." He paused and held his hands up in a helpless gesture. "Frankly, Claudia, you worry me. I fear that the next time I find you, you'll be hurt, or I'll hear you've been sent back to America because your grandfather found out what you've been doing."

Her eyes widened with anxiety. "You're not going to tell him, are you? If he finds out, he'll take me to Scotland and marry me off to some burly highlander with bad manners. And I can't—"

Cameron pressed his finger over her lips. "What are you talking about? What highlander?"

She grabbed his hand and moved it from her mouth. "*Any* highlander—it doesn't matter! He's always vexed with me, Cameron, and if he knows I've dressed like a boy and risked my life to look for my—well, look for someone—he'll marry me off, and I'll have to live in the mountains where it snows all the time and—"

"Claudia, if you will calm down—"

"No, no! You must not—"

He kissed her again.

❧

It occurred to Cameron, as he caressed her lips with his own, he could have found other ways to calm her down.

This one, however, seemed the most enjoyable.

He cupped her face gently and was happily surprised when she began to kiss him back. But as much as he wanted to continue, he knew he must act honorably. Slowly he lifted his head, breaking the kiss, and watched her eyes open slowly.

He didn't know how she would react once she had her wits about her, and he truly expected her to be upset again.

He should have known Claudia never reacted as one might expect.

"You kissed me—again," she said, her voice sounding confused.

"Umm," he agreed. "I did say it might happen again."

"Yes, but it isn't at all proper."

He grinned, one hand still holding her cheek. "Because we're not betrothed."

"Exactly," she said, finally backing away from him. "I don't understand why you keep doing it."

Cameron sighed and wondered that very thing himself. He usually had much better control. "Neither do I," he finally admitted aloud.

Claudia bit her lip as her gaze searched his face. "I believe I got dirt on your cheek."

Cameron reached up and felt the dirt dusted on the side of his face and wiped it away. He'd kissed a few women in his life, but this was the strangest conversation he'd ever had after the kiss was over.

He almost laughed aloud but noticed that Claudia seemed ill at ease, so he held it in and motioned toward her chair again. "Why don't you sit down and tell me whom you've gone to so much trouble to find?"

She did as he asked but seemed reluctant to talk. "It's not important. You never did tell me what you are doing here, though, and what this place is."

Cameron pulled a chair over and sat in front of her. He was determined to get the information out of her. "You tell me your story first."

Claudia let out a breath. "I came because someone told me I might find my grandfather down here."

"The marquis?" Cameron asked.

She shook her head. "No. My mother's father. No one will tell me where he lives, especially my grandfather Moreland. But I did hear that he or someone who may know him might be down here by the river."

Cameron suddenly understood why she'd gone to so much trouble. He might have done the same thing had he been in her shoes. "Tell me his name, and I might be able to help you find him."

"Well, his name is—" She stopped and looked at him. "Wait one minute. That's why you kissed me, isn't it? You knew it would make me"—she waved her hand about in the air—"befuddled, and I would pour out my story to you."

Cameron was taken aback by the sudden change in her mood as she sprang from her chair. He watched her grab the dirty cap off the desk, jam it on her head, and begin stuffing her russet locks under it.

He stood quickly and took hold of her hands. "That's not why I kissed you. I—"

"Excuse me, my lord. Is everything all right?" Cameron recognized the voice as his butler's.

He turned to find George standing in the doorway eyeing the ragged figure before him. "Everything is fine, George," he assured him.

"Do I need to get another bed ready?" George persisted, still looking at Claudia as if she were a thief or a beggar.

"No, I was about to give her. . .er. . .*him* a ride home."

He put his hand on Claudia's back to move her toward the door. But when they got closer, one long dark strand of her hair fell out from underneath the cap. Her eyes wide, she deftly pushed it back and hurried out the door.

"Is that a—"

"Yes, it's a girl."

"Is it the same—"

"Yes. Same girl."

George cleared his throat and lifted his head to look straight ahead. "Very peculiar, my lord."

Cameron clapped his butler on the shoulder. "You have no idea, George." He started to leave and then turned back. "You won't tell anyone—"

"Not an utterance, my lord."

"Excellent," Cameron murmured, feeling awkward, and stepped out into the hallway.

When he didn't see Claudia right away he hurried into the main area, only to find her standing there observing what was happening in the room.

The ladies had finished eating, and some were sewing garments and hats while several children were singing a song. Still another group was sitting at a table being shown how to put a menu together. They were learning ways to make a living once they left the shelter.

"Shall we go?" Cameron asked, coming alongside of her.

For once she had nothing to say; she only nodded and made her way to the door.

When they were inside the buggy she spoke. "You're running a charity for women and children."

It wasn't a question, but Cameron answered anyway. "Yes. I told you after the ball that I echoed your sentiments about finding God's will for my life and doing something to benefit others."

Another strand of hair fell out from under her cap, but she tucked it behind her ear. "I thought you were only trying to impress me."

"Hmm. That seems a near impossible task where you are concerned."

She frowned at him. "Well, you don't seem to be trying hard at all. You're either scolding me or kissing me!"

Cameron's eyes widened. "If you'll remember correctly I've saved your life. Twice! And I've yet to hear you say thank you."

"Twice?" she gasped. "I was doing fine with that mugger until you came along and caused him to scar my arm, and I was about to turn and go home today when you scared me to death by chasing me down like a criminal." She let out a sharp breath, folded her arms, and looked away from him.

The woman was making him crazy! "Perhaps it is wise for your grandfather to marry you off to a Scotsman. For then I wouldn't have to worry about what insane scheme you'd come up with next!" He felt silly trading insults with a woman he only wanted to know better.

But with Claudia, might a man have a normal courtship?

"We can save each other any worry on that score by simply avoiding one another. I know I shall endeavor to avoid you like the plague."

Cameron let out a sigh and refused to let himself be baited. "Do you want me to take you to your home?" he asked instead.

"Oh, no!" she cried. "Just take me to the Duke of Northingshire's home, if you please."

Cameron glanced at her. "Perhaps that might not be the best course of action. North might be upset and forbid his wife to continue your association if he spots how you are dressed."

Claudia glared at him again. "North would never forbid his wife anything because he loves and respects her. I'm sure he didn't go about kissing her before they became engaged. And anyway—"

"We could become engaged, you know, if this is what's troubling you," he said, smiling.

"I would rather marry a Scotsman!" she returned.

Cameron smiled again and led her out to his conveyance. When they were almost to the duke's home, he slowed the buggy to a stop. "You might want to get out here and go in by the back entrance."

She nodded, and before he could come around to help her down she was walking toward the house.

"Will you be at the Lamptons' ball on Friday?" he called after her.

"Not if you're going to be there," she shot back and kept walking.

Cameron chuckled as he watched the tattered figure disappear into the Northingshires' shrubbery.

He'd prayed God would send him the perfect woman. He had no idea God would think he needed such a difficult one.

But every minute he spent in Claudia's presence, no matter how exasperating she could be, it made him want her in his life even more.

As he climbed back into his buggy, he remembered how fascinated she'd been by his shelter, the way she'd smiled at the children who were busy with their lessons.

If Claudia were his wife, he knew he'd have not only someone to love, but someone to share his dreams, too.

Now if he could just figure out how to convince her they were perfect for one another.

six

It wasn't easy for Claudia to sneak into the servants' entrance of Northingshire Manor and get upstairs without the servants seeing her. But she finally arrived at Helen's room and entered without knocking.

The moment Claudia saw Helen standing by her wardrobe, she ran and threw her arms around her. "Oh, I'm so glad you're here—," she began but stopped when she realized Helen was not hugging her back but pounding on her arms trying to get free.

And then she screamed.

Claudia took hold of Helen's flailing arms. "Helen! It's me, Claudia!" she cried and was relieved when Helen finally looked her in the face and stopped fighting her.

"Claudia?" she gasped. "Why are you dressed like a boy?"

"Well, I—"

"Stand away from her now!" a man's voice boomed from the doorway.

Claudia whirled to see North, Helen's husband, coming toward her with a fierce frown on his face.

"Helllennn!" Claudia squealed as she stepped behind her friend, using her as a shield.

"What—" North started to reach around Helen, but his wife held out her arms to stop him.

"North! It's Claudia! Calm down!" Helen exclaimed.

North glanced at his wife then glared at Claudia again.

"North! It's me, Claudia. See?" She tore off her cap and let her hair fall about her shoulders.

North's glare turned into a look of astonishment, and then he

53

burst into laughter. "Whatever possessed you to don these rags?"

Claudia sighed and stepped out from behind Helen. "It seemed like a good idea at the time." She told them of her trip down to the wharf and her search for her grandfather.

Helen put her hand to her chest. "Oh, Claudia! What if someone recognized you?"

Claudia looked at her friend sheepishly. "Well, I'm afraid someone did. Lord Kinclary."

North raised his brows in surprise. "Isn't Kinclary the one who saved you from the mugger?"

Claudia nodded. She had told them both what had happened the day before. "Yes, and he takes great delight in thinking he's saved my life twice now. The man is arrogant and insufferable."

Helen's eyes took on a dreamy look. "I knew he had to be a good man. He's your conquering hero!" She sighed.

Claudia frowned at her overdramatic friend. "No, he's more like a thorn in my side," she stated dryly.

"Well, I like Kinclary. There was some bad blood between him and my friends, the Thornton brothers, but that was all settled when Thomas Thornton married Cameron's sister Katherine." North shrugged. "I've become better acquainted with him since he's been back in town, and I like him. He's even started a shelter, which I've donated to, although he likes to keep it a secret."

"Yes, I already know about the shelter. I was there today," Claudia said. "But it still doesn't excuse the fact that he's exceedingly rude. Do you know he yelled at me? Twice!"

North laughed, making both women frown at him. "I'm sorry, but it sounds as if you're going to lead poor Kinclary on a bigger adventure than Helen did me while we were courting."

"North!" Helen admonished

"I'm not leading him anywhere!" Claudia exclaimed. "And we are not courting."

Apparently North wasn't convinced. He shook his head and continued to laugh on his way down the hallway.

"Oh, don't listen to him." Helen took Claudia's hand and led her to the cushioned window seat. "So tell me everything—especially the romantic parts."

Claudia looked away. "What makes you think there is anything romantic between us?" she asked as evenly as she could.

"Because you blushed when you declared you weren't courting," Helen stated matter-of-factly.

Claudia glanced at her friend then blurted out, "He kissed me."

"What?" Helen gasped. "When?"

Claudia knew if she didn't tell someone she'd burst. "After he apprehended that mugger and then today after he dragged me off the street."

Helen's eyes widened. "He's kissed you twice? You're not even betrothed."

"That's what I told him," Claudia threw her arms up in exasperation. "Of course I slapped him the first time he did it."

Helen nodded thoughtfully. "What did you do the second time?"

Claudia could feel her cheeks burning as she looked away again. "I. . .uh. . .well, it's not important," she stammered. "The point is, Helen, I have promised myself that I shall never see him again. It is a promise I intend to keep."

A strange expression passed over Helen's face. "That might not be possible," she said.

Claudia shook her head. "What do you mean?"

"Well, I've been checking with my staff, and I"—she paused, her eyes shining—"I found your grandfather Canterbury."

Claudia's heart pounded faster. "Wh—where is he?"

Helen winced. "Well, that part is a bit sticky. You see your grandfather is working as a butler to—" She paused again as if she were afraid to speak her next words.

Claudia grabbed her hand. "Whoever it is matters not to me, Helen. Just speak it."

"He's working for Lord Kinclary," Helen said in one fast breath.

Claudia pulled her hand back slowly, her mind whirling with the implications of Helen's news. She didn't know what to say. "It makes me want to laugh and cry at the same time," she murmured, bringing her gaze up to meet Helen's. She fell silent again then finally said, "I think I may have met my grandfather, and I didn't even know it." She shook her head. "How could I not recognize my own grandfather?"

Helen reached out and patted her arm. "Don't worry about that now. You must concentrate your efforts on figuring out a way to tell Kinclary your news."

Claudia stood and paced. "I am the granddaughter of his butler, Helen. Cameron is the future Duke of Ravenhurst, tenth in line to the throne."

Helen stepped in front of her to stop her pacing. "Why does it matter? I thought you didn't want to have anything to do with Kinclary," she reminded her gently.

Claudia shook her head. "I don't. It's only—well, he might not want to help me get to know my grandfather Canterbury once he realizes the truth. It might change his perception of me."

Helen smiled at her gently. "Claudia, it seems to me, no matter how much you deny it, the two of you have feelings for one another. I'm sure he already knows the story of your parents' elopement. Why would this make a difference?"

Claudia could not deny Helen's assessment, for it was true. But would those feelings continue once he found out the truth?

❧

"I don't understand where he could be!" Claudia waved her hands about in the air. "A week has passed, and I've attended three balls. Why doesn't he show himself?"

She leaned back in Helen's carriage and stared up at the gray velvet ceiling. Helen, sitting across from her, reached out to pat her knee.

"I'm sure something has come up to detain him. Don't lose hope yet. Once you speak to him today, I'm sure everything will turn out all right."

"Are you sure we're doing the right thing by going to his home? What if he thinks I'm pursuing him or something?" she said anxiously.

Helen gave her a level look. "After what you told him the last time you parted, I don't believe he thinks you're marriage minded," she answered dryly.

Claudia thought back to that day and became even more concerned. "Perhaps I've offended him. He seemed fine when I left, but later he might have thought about what I said and become angry with me."

"Stop fretting," Helen admonished as the carriage came to a stop. "Now let's put on our best smiles, walk in that house, and tell Kinclary our news. God will guide us, I'm sure."

Claudia had faith in God; she just wasn't sure about Cameron.

After a few moments they were standing at the large door, banging with the ring held by the giant lion's head.

When the door opened, Claudia was disappointed to find her grandfather was not the one behind it. "We're here to see Lord Kinclary," she told the servant, hoping her nervousness did not show.

The young servant eyed the two of them. "Do you have an appointment?"

"No, but you can tell him that Lady Claudia is here to see him about a most urgent matter." She hoped the mysteriousness of her statement would cause him to let her in.

The man hesitated a moment, then showed them into the large entrance hall. "Please wait here while I take him your message." He motioned for them to sit on a delicate settee by the door.

As they waited, Claudia could only stare straight ahead and concentrate on being calm.

"Just look at these paintings, Claudia. I'll bet they are worth a fortune." She pointed to the ceiling. "And have you ever seen such a large chandelier? Amazing!"

"Helen, please!" Claudia whispered. "Reminding me of how rich and powerful he is does not help to calm my poor nerves."

Helen started to speak but stopped when Cameron suddenly walked into the foyer. He looked at Claudia first, and the smile that lit his face nearly took her breath away. "Lady Claudia." His deep voice resembled smooth honey as he walked toward them. "What a pleasant surprise."

"I don't think he's angry," Helen whispered.

"Shh!" Claudia gave her friend a gentle nudge with her elbow.

"Lord Kinclary," she greeted him in return. "You know my friend, Lady Northingshire?"

She was relieved when he turned to Helen with a warm smile. "Ah, yes. I believe our introduction was interrupted in the park. I'm so glad to finally make your acquaintance." He picked up her gloved hand and bent over it gallantly.

Helen put her other hand to her chest, and Claudia had to bite her lip to hide a smile. Helen was such a romantic, and now she would be talking about his courtly behavior for weeks.

Cameron escorted them into a brightly lit parlor and seated them on a brocade-covered sofa. After ringing for tea he sat across from them. "Now to what do I owe the pleasure of this visit?"

He smiled at her confidently, as if he found her presence in his home no surprise at all.

"This is not a sociable call. We've come only to inquire after a certain matter," she informed him abruptly.

Cameron's smile deepened. "Are you sure you're not here because you missed me?"

"Preposterous!"

"That's partly the reason," Helen affirmed at the same time as Claudia denied it.

"Helen!" Claudia admonished.

"Well?" Helen said with a shrug.

"Or did you finally want to thank me for those rescues?"

"No," she snapped but then decided to soften her tone a bit. She was here, after all, to ask for his help. "I mean, of course, I thank you for rescuing me from that horrid mugger, but it isn't why I—"

"Wait one minute!" he interrupted her then turned to Helen. "You are a witness to this statement, are you not? She *did* just thank me? I'm not dreaming?"

Helen giggled as she nodded, and Claudia closed her eyes briefly, praying for patience. "Lord Kinclary—"

"Cameron," he corrected.

She pursed her lips and shook her head. *"Cameron."* She wasn't going to argue the point. "We're not here because I've missed you or any other such nonsense." She ignored his look of disbelief and hurried to say the rest. "I'm here because I found out where my grandfather is, and only *you* can help me meet him."

Cameron's flirtatious smile turned questioning. "I don't understand."

Claudia exchanged a glance with Helen then looked back to him. "My grandfather is—" Claudia swallowed nervously. Her throat was so dry she nearly choked. She suddenly stood up. "Perhaps this is not the best time to go into all this. I think we should leave. Now!"

Helen stood with her and took hold of her arm. "Just tell him."

Claudia glanced at Cameron and found she could not say it. It *did* matter to her what he thought of her. She *did* have feelings for him, which went deeper than she wanted to admit.

If telling him meant he might look down upon her, she didn't think she could bear it. "I can't. We must leave."

Helen shook her head as Cameron stood up with them. "Lord Kinclary, Claudia's grandfather is George Canterbury—your butler."

When he didn't say anything, Claudia finally let her gaze rise to see his expression. He appeared absolutely stunned.

Claudia's heart dropped when he glanced at her before looking away. "Are you sure it's my George Canterbury?"

"Yes. He was a butler in Grandfather Moreland's home when my father married his daughter," Claudia answered stiffly. Her fears were coming to fruition when Cameron still would not look at her.

"Lord Kinclary," Helen cut in, "could you perhaps speak to your butler and ask if he would meet with Claudia? Her greatest desire is to form a relationship with him."

Cameron nodded slowly. "Of course. I'll speak to him directly," he murmured, almost absently.

Claudia couldn't take it anymore. "Well, we've wasted enough of your time, Lord Kinclary. We must be going," she announced starchily as she marched past him with her head held high.

"Claudia!" he called after her, but she walked even faster and left the room.

She could hear Helen's footsteps behind her, and soon they were both climbing into the carriage. "Claudia! Will you please wait a moment?" Cameron called as he ran out of the house and toward the carriage.

Claudia ignored him and knocked on the ceiling, letting the driver know to start moving.

She tried not to, but she found herself peeking out the window at him. She started when she found herself looking right into his eyes. But before she could read his expression she let the curtain fall back into place and willed herself not to cry.

seven

Cameron watched the carriage drive away, aware that Claudia had taken his reaction for censure. Of course he knew her mother had not been highborn, but it was shocking to find that George, a man he'd come to rely on as not only an employee but a good friend, was the grandfather of the woman he was growing fond of.

He was not a snobbish man, but having been born surrounded by servants it was hard to reconcile that they could someday be a part of his family.

George Canterbury had been in his father's household for years and his own for the last six months. He had volunteered to help Cameron renovate the warehouse and then manage it because he'd said he had a desire to help others also. It had never occurred to him to ask his butler anything about his past, and George had never offered the information.

Before speaking to him, however, he wanted to know more about what had happened. The only other person Cameron knew who might tell him was his mother. She would be only too happy to pass along any information she may have.

The next day he took his carriage and rode up to Ravenhurst Castle where his parents had retired after the ball.

"Cameron!" his mother greeted him as if she hadn't seen him in years. "Why have you come?" she asked then sucked in her breath. "You've become engaged, haven't you? Tell me—is it Lady Claudia? The two of you seem very well suited—"

"Mother!" He held out his hand. "I'm not engaged to anyone. I've come on another matter, and we'll speak of Lady Claudia after that."

The smile faded slightly from his mother's face. "Well, come into the parlor and tell me all. Your father is out in the back field shooting birds. Should I fetch him?" She walked over to the satin cord, used to ring for the servants, but he stopped her.

"No. I'll talk to him later. It's you I wanted to see."

Lady Ravenhurst smiled again as she sat down and motioned for him to do the same.

"Mother, can you tell me how George Canterbury came to be in our family's employ?" he asked once they were seated comfortably.

His mother frowned. "This is what you want to talk about? What does this have to do with Claudia?"

He shook his head and hoped his mother could focus on the conversation. "I'll tell you about Claudia in a moment. Just tell me about George."

His mother sighed. "It was the Marquis of Moreland, Claudia's grandfather, who recommended him to us. We needed a butler for our summer home in Bath." She shrugged as if the whole topic of servants was beneath her. "That is where he was, as you know, when your father sent him to your house."

Cameron nodded. "I see." He thought about how George must have felt losing his job with Claudia's grandfather. Knowing the marquis, he'd want to get rid of any remembrance of his son's disappointing marriage. Why then, he wondered, did he allow Claudia to come live with him and become his heir?

"Cameron!" his mother snapped. When he glanced up at her, he realized she must have been trying to get his attention for a while. "Will you pay attention?"

"I'm sorry, Mother. You were saying?"

She let out a sharp breath. "I asked you why you are so interested in your butler. It's not wise, son, to get too chummy with one's servants, you know. They might take advantage."

"Mother," he said wearily, "I don't need a lecture on proper employer protocol. I only wanted to know about him, nothing more. I would have asked him, but I didn't want him to think I mistrusted or suspected him of something."

His mother often chose not to see beyond the surface of things. It was too much of a bother, especially if it had nothing to do with her own life and well-being. But on this particular day, unfortunately, she chose to surprise him.

"What does George have to do with Claudia?"

Cameron did not want her to know George was Claudia's grandfather. She knew about Claudia's mother being a servant's daughter, but she didn't know the particulars. She might think it would cause a lot of talk and speculation if this information were to reach the ton's ears.

"Nothing. I did want to tell you, however, that I'm about to begin calling on her."

"Splendid! I had hoped that—" His mother stopped and narrowed her gaze at Cameron. "Wait a moment. You're asking about George because you believe he has a connection to Claudia."

Cameron looked away and mentally measured the distance between him and the door. "I'm not asking anything, Mother. I never said one had to do with the other."

She wagged her finger at him. "George came into our employ about the time Moreland disinherited his son." Suddenly she clutched her hand to her chest. "Oh, no! Please tell me Claudia is not your butler's granddaughter?"

"I think I'll go speak to Father before I leave." He ignored his mother's request, quickly crossing the room to the door.

"Cameron! You must reconsider this match. We will be the laughingstock of all London if this gets out," she called after him, but he was closing the door behind him.

That he thought his mother wouldn't put two and two together was evidence his encounters with Claudia were making him a bit muddleheaded.

He kept walking until he reached the back of the estate where his father was shooting at birds but not hitting one of them.

The duke, with rifle pointed to the sky, glanced at his son and nodded to his left. "Grab a rifle, Son. Perhaps you can hit something. My eyes don't seem to focus anymore."

Cameron shook his head and smiled as his father took another shot. "If you would wear your spectacles, you might be eating pheasant tonight."

Lord Ravenhurst frowned and squinted at the sky. "Bah! It bothers me to have something sit on my nose. I can get along just capital without them."

His father's rifle rang out again. Cameron looked up at the sky and saw the birds circling overhead as if they knew they were not in danger.

Finally his father put aside his gun and sat down with a heavy sigh. Once he'd taken a drink of lemonade, which was waiting for him on the table, his mood seemed to improve. "So what brings you to Ravenhurst?"

Cameron sat down and leaned back in the chair. "I wanted to find out more about my butler, George."

"Ah," he nodded, taking another drink. "You must have found out that Lady Claudia is his granddaughter."

"You knew?" Cameron asked, surprised.

"Moreland came to me when he heard I was searching about trying to find a butler for our home in Bath. He told me what had happened and then made me pledge to keep the matter quiet. As a matter of fact, George wasn't thrilled about the match either," he added. "If you're thinking about approaching him about this, he might not be cooperative."

Cameron frowned; he hadn't considered this possibility. "But I promised Claudia I would arrange a meeting between them."

"So this is the way the wind blows, does it?" His father eyed him keenly.

"Yes, and I have to try with George because this is something that is very important to Claudia."

"If you marry the girl, it will present a problem having her own grandfather as her butler. You could, of course, have him run that shelter of yours and act as its president."

Cameron jerked his gaze back to his father. "You know about the shelter?"

"When I was alerted to how much money you were spending, I had to find out if you were gambling away your legacy or spending it in some other unsavory pursuit," his father said. "You could have told me, you know."

Cameron winced at the censure and hurt in his father's voice. He had spent so much time away from home that he didn't know his father well at all and couldn't say how he might have reacted. He should have known the duke would be keeping an eye on his son's portion. "I see that now," he admitted. "I find great reward in working there."

"You're a good boy, Cameron. You always were. I'm sorry I didn't spend more time with you. It was just the way of things, you know."

Cameron looked into his father's eyes and saw the remorse there. The firstborn sons were usually sent off to school at a young age so they could prepare for their titles. He would come home at holidays, but even then his father was usually busy with his estates or serving in the House of Lords. "I understood," he told him truthfully. It was, indeed, the way every one of his friends had been brought up.

But it was not how his children would be reared. He vowed to make sure of it.

"Raven?" Cameron heard his mother call, and the two men exchanged a look. It was the look most men wore when they knew their masculine solitude was about to be invaded by a female. "Is Cameron with you? I need to speak with him immediately."

His father's brow furrowed. "Tell me you did not say anything to your mother about George and Claudia being related."

Cameron grimaced. "I'm afraid she guessed."

His father shook his head. "Well, you'd better hurry on then. I'll stall her as best I can."

Cameron shared a grin with his father before making a run for his carriage. His escape was halted, however, when he found his sixteen-year-old sister, Lucy, waiting for him by the vehicle.

"Lucy!" He stumbled backward from the impact of her overeager hug. "I thought you were with Katherine at Rosehaven."

She backed away a bit and gave him a dramatic, forlorn expression. "I was, but Tyler keeps getting into all my things and hiding them, and Katherine is so busy with the baby that she doesn't have time to spend with me."

"Well, Tyler is only four, and I'm sure Katherine appreciated your playing with him while she is so busy."

She grabbed his hand and looked up into his face. "Can't I come and stay with you? I don't want to wait to have my coming out next year. I want to go to balls and meet handsome young men. If I wait too long, they might all be taken."

Cameron hid a grin while he observed his little sister for the first time since he'd been home. She had become quite a beauty, with her golden red hair and her fair complexion. His parents were going to be put on a merry ride when this one stepped out into the world. "I promise there will be young men to spare next year, and you shouldn't be so anxious to grow up. You have plenty of time for that."

Lucy sighed and dropped his hand. "No one truly understands me. I feel like the princess locked in the glass tower. The only places I ever get to go are church and Rosehaven," she declared, throwing her arms wide.

Cameron couldn't hold back his chuckle as he patted her on the head. "Your time will come and—"

"Cameron!" his mother's voice called to him from a distance.

"Sorry, but I have to go," he told Lucy then jumped into his carriage. "I'll talk to you soon," he promised before shutting the door.

"If only I could leave as easily as you!" he heard her cry as his carriage began to roll away.

It was afternoon before he could return to the shelter and speak with his butler. After what his father told him, he wasn't so confident the meeting would go as he'd hoped it would.

And he was right.

"I'm sorry, sir, but it's best for all if my granddaughter and I do *not* meet. She'll never be accepted by the ton if she openly acknowledges me as a relative. And if Moreland finds out, I'm afraid he'll cut her off as he did the girl's father," George told Cameron.

"Claudia has gone to great lengths to find you—believe me! She's willing to risk the ton *and* Moreland to know you."

George turned away from him and went to stand by the window. "I'm sorry, my lord, but I prefer not to meet with her."

Frustrated by his butler's stubbornness, Cameron told him the truth. "You've already met her, George. But neither of you knew who the other one was."

George whirled to face him. "When would I have. . ." His voice drifted off, and his eyes widened. "She isn't the young woman you brought home the other night, is she?"

Cameron nodded. "Yes, she is."

"And she's the same one who was dressed in those tattered clothes you were yelling at in your office?" he said carefully.

Cameron smiled sheepishly. "I wasn't exactly yelling, but, yes, she's the one."

Cameron took a step back when he saw George's face redden with anger. "I thought she might be a trollop, the way you spent so much time alone with her! Where was her chaperone, and why were you kissing her?"

Cameron opened and closed his mouth. What plausible explanation could he give? "Your granddaughter has a penchant for getting herself into messes, which I've had to save her from twice." He knew he should say no more, but he couldn't keep from asking, "And how did you know I kissed her?"

"How else would you have gotten dirt on your face?"

Cameron winced and lowered his gaze. "I know I might have been out of line—"

"Have you compromised her?" George charged.

"No!" Cameron exclaimed. "I have only the best intentions toward Claudia. I hope to win her hand."

George grew quieter then. "Even more reason for us not to acknowledge our family connections." With that he walked out of the room, leaving Cameron to wonder what he was going to do.

❧

He was late. For the fourth time in only five minutes Claudia paused before the clock on the parlor mantle and sighed as she resumed pacing.

Cameron had sent a note to her the night before, saying he would come by at ten. It was now ten thirty, and he had still not come.

"Stop your pacing, girl!" her grandfather ordered, walking into the parlor. He noticed what she was wearing and grunted. "You're not dressed as if you're about to greet a beau."

Claudia dropped into a chair and smoothed the skirt of her gray morning dress. "He's not my beau, and I'm certainly not dressing to impress *him*."

Her grandfather crossed the room to where she sat and scowled down at her. "Not a beau? Then what is his business here this morning if not to come calling?"

"He's simply a friend—that's all." She glanced once more at the clock.

"Humph! You certainly seem anxious because he hasn't arrived yet, and I can't imagine any young gentleman visiting a lady only because he wants to be friends."

"Grandfather—," she began but was interrupted by their butler announcing Lord Kinclary had arrived.

Claudia anxiously watched Cameron step into the room and greet her grandfather. She tried to read his expression but was unable to decipher what he might be thinking.

"So you're Kinclary," her grandfather said in his gruff way while making a show of sizing up Cameron.

"Yes, Lord Moreland," Cameron answered with a quick bow of his head. "Thank you for allowing me to meet with your granddaughter this morning."

"Yes, well, don't let her American traits dampen your interest. I'm sure with enough time spent here in England she'll come around to the way of things."

"Grandfather!" Claudia exclaimed. "I told you we are not—"

"Be assured, Lord Moreland," Cameron interrupted, sending her a mysterious glance. "I find her American ways part of her charm."

Claudia rolled her eyes and folded her arms as she watched the pleased smile crease her grandfather's face. Had she ever seen him smile?

"Capital!" Her grandfather slapped Cameron on his shoulder. "Well, my sister, Lady Julia, is here to chaperone, so I'll leave you two to. . ." He waved his hand about and left the room.

Cameron looked at Claudia before turning to her aunt Julia sitting quietly in the corner of the room doing needlepoint. "Lady Julia," he greeted her.

Her aunt glanced up, gave him a vague smile, then went back to her stitching.

"Aunt Julia can't hear very well, so you can be sure she won't repeat our conversation," Claudia told him.

Finally Cameron turned his full attention on her and smiled gently. Claudia's heart picked up its pace when she realized he seemed pleased to see her.

"Claudia." He stepped in front of her. "I'm sorry I'm late. I had to attend to a situation at the shelter."

She motioned to the chair behind him and sat back down. "Please have a seat." Once he was seated, she wasted no time in getting to the subject. "Have you spoken to my grandfather?"

He hesitated, and Claudia's heart sank. "Yes, but he refuses to see you."

Tears filled Claudia's eyes, and she blinked rapidly to keep them from falling. "But—why?"

Cameron reached inside his coat and handed her his handkerchief. "He feels it would hurt your standing with the ton. I told him you didn't care about that, but he seems to think keeping himself separate from you is for the best."

"But it's not for the best," she insisted quietly so as not to startle her aunt. "He is my grandfather. Shouldn't he want to know me?"

Cameron nodded. "I believe he does, Claudia, but the rules of conduct for a servant are hard for a man of his years to overlook. When his daughter married your father, it upset not only Moreland but George, as well. Your parents broke the rules, and neither of your grandfathers knew how to deal with it."

Claudia thought about his words; having dealt with servants all her life, she knew he was right. "But what can I do? There has to be a way to let him know I *want* to be recognized as his granddaughter. I'd be proud to know him better."

Cameron leaned over, his elbows braced on his knees. "What if I told you I had a plan?" he whispered.

Claudia found herself leaning over, too. "I'll do anything!"

"It would require you to spend a lot of time with me," he warned.

Looking into his sparkling green eyes, Claudia could not see this as a negative point. "I can abide it, if you can."

Cameron smiled widely and leaned back in his chair. "Excellent. Now this is what we need to do—," he began and filled her in on his plan.

eight

Cameron couldn't believe how perfect his plan was. Having Claudia work with him at the shelter would not only allow her to get to know her grandfather but enable him to spend time with the woman of his dreams.

What surprised him was that she didn't even hesitate to agree. She'd told him it was exactly the kind of charitable work she'd been looking for, and spending time with her grandfather, no matter how much he could ignore her, was better than no time at all.

The only problem in their plan was that she couldn't very well bring Aunt Julia along with her, so they decided to enlist the help of Helen and North to bring her to the shelter.

Before Cameron left Claudia's house, he made an appointment to meet her and the Northingshires in Hyde Park at three.

Now, as Cameron paced about the park waiting for her to arrive, he thought about how his feelings for her had grown.

Had a woman ever plagued his heart and mind so sweetly as this American beauty? She made him feel so many emotions when he gazed at her, and many feelings he didn't understand.

One important thing he was aware of, though, was that God had answered his prayer. He had desired to meet a woman who had a zeal for helping others and loved God as he did.

Claudia had these qualities and so much more. She could fascinate and aggravate him all within a matter of minutes; yet he enjoyed every minute.

"Cameron!" He heard a voice calling him and smiled even before he turned and saw Claudia coming toward him with the Duke and Duchess of Northingshire.

"Hello, Claudia. Your graces." He greeted them all with a casual bow.

North stepped up and held out his hand. "Good to see you, Kinclary. I saw your sister a fortnight ago and was glad to note your new niece takes after her mother and not her ugly father!"

Cameron chuckled as he shook North's hand. "Don't let Katherine hear you say that. She is quite smug in the fact that she thinks her husband the most handsome catch in all of England." The men shared a laugh, and then Cameron turned to Claudia.

"Did you tell them the reason for this meeting?"

Claudia nodded. "Yes, and they are willing to help get me to the shelter and make sure Grandfather Moreland knows nothing about it for now."

"Actually we want to do more than just bring Claudia to the shelter," North spoke up, putting his arm around his wife. "Our lives have felt a little empty since we moved from Louisiana. Being involved in charitable work to help others is both our hearts' desire. We'd love to stay and help you."

"I could certainly use your help and *your connections*," Cameron assured him, adding the last part with a grin.

North laughed. "Excellent! Then we'll see you on Monday."

They started to walk away, but Cameron stopped them. "Would you mind if I spoke to Claudia alone for a few minutes? It concerns her grandfather."

North looked from Cameron to Claudia, then smiled at his wife. "We'll be over by the pond when you're ready."

Once they were out of hearing distance, Claudia looked at Cameron. "Has something happened?"

"It is something I should have told you earlier—rather *warned* you about." He took a deep breath. "My mother knows about George being your grandfather."

Claudia looked at him, a puzzled expression on her face. "Did you tell her?"

"No, but I went to her for information about George, and I'm afraid she came to the conclusion on her own."

"I don't follow what you're saying," Claudia said. "How did she connect me with my grandfather George?"

Cameron gazed at her and found himself wishing she hadn't worn such a large bonnet. It covered too much of her beautiful hair. "As you know, she's hinted at a match between you and me. And when she saw how long we spoke at the ball, she assumed I'd begun calling on you."

Claudia's gaze flew to his. "You denied this, of course?"

Cameron grinned. "No, I didn't." She opened her mouth, no doubt to reprimand him, but he continued before she could say anything. "But you know my mother as well as anyone. She's a terrible snob, Claudia, and I'm afraid she wasn't thrilled about your connection with George Canterbury."

"But I thought everyone knew my mother was a servant's daughter."

Cameron tried to think of a reasonable way to excuse his mother's behavior but couldn't. "It was fine when he was an unknown servant in some other person's employ; but it's quite a different story when he has been her servant and now my own."

"I see," she murmured, lowering her head and shielding her face with her bonnet.

He could tell she didn't *see* at all. "Claudia, my mother can be silly and vain at times, but her opinion is hers alone."

"But you were thinking the same thing, weren't you, when you first heard the truth?" she charged, popping her head back up and nearly hitting him with the rim of her bonnet.

"What?" he exclaimed, letting out a breath. "I thought no such thing!"

"But you could hardly look at me!"

"I was surprised by the news, Claudia," he replied. "And I was upset with myself when I realized I didn't know my butler—who has become a friend, I might add—as well as I thought."

Claudia took a breath, then folded her arms in front of her. "Well, it matters not whether your mother or anyone else thinks my connections too low for you, Lord Kinclary," she told him stiffly. "We are not courting, as your mother thought, so it is a moot point."

Cameron noticed the high color which had arisen on her cheeks was the same color as the lovely gown she was wearing. "Why do you always do that?"

"Do what?"

"Become so defensive with me. Is this an American trait, or do you just feel uncomfortable around me?"

She unfolded her arms and propped her hands on her waist. "I'm not *de*fensive; I'm mostly *of*fended! And would you please stop blaming everything I do on my American upbringing?"

His eyes widened. "I offended you?"

She sighed. "Well, perhaps that is the wrong word. Confused is closer to the truth." She began to pace. "I've never had a man yell at me, scold me, flirt with me, protect me, tease me about becoming engaged, and, on top of everything else, kiss me! Frankly I don't how to act when I'm around you."

Cameron smiled as she counted off each item on her fingers. If the lady only knew how much confusion he felt every time he was near her! But he'd keep that little fact to himself. There was no sense in letting her know he wasn't in complete control of his emotions where she was concerned.

Not yet anyway.

"We've had quite an adventurous beginning to our friendship, have we not?" he said instead.

She stopped her pacing, looked at him, then burst into laughter. "That is putting it mildly!" She laughed again, and Cameron chuckled with her. "Even my meeting the famous pirate Jean Lafitte does not compare."

He stopped laughing. "How would a young lady even be in the vicinity of such a criminal? Surely your father would not allow it?" he charged, his mind conjuring all sorts of scenarios and none of them pleasant.

She laughed again, clearly enjoying his irritation. "He didn't know!" she told him, her voice full of mischief. "Good day, my lord."

She was uttering her last words as she walked away from him.

"Claudia—," he began but stopped when he realized other people were standing around.

He was still watching when she glanced back at him and grinned. It was only for a moment, but it made him forget his irritation and put a smile on his face.

It suddenly occurred to him that he was falling in love with a woman who counted Indians and pirates among her acquaintances.

God truly must have a sense of humor, he thought.

⁂

The next morning, because she had stayed the night at the Northingshires' house, Claudia walked with Helen and North to church.

She glanced down at her peach gown and adjusted the bow tied on the high waistline. After that she smoothed down her skirts and reached up to fidget with her matching peach bonnet.

"Claudia, you look fine," Helen leaned over to whisper in her ear. "And I'm sure Kinclary will concur."

Claudia tried to look as though she had no idea what Helen was talking about. "Oh, really? I didn't know he went to our church."

Helen elbowed her. "What a short memory you have since we saw him there last Sunday!"

Claudia grinned at her friend. "All right—I did know. But I care nothing about what he thinks of my dress."

"I must say it is fortunate we're going to church this morning since it seems you will need to repent of all your lies!"

Claudia put her hand over her mouth to hide her smile. "Nonsense," she murmured when they reached the heavy wooden door to the church.

As they walked to their seats, they greeted various friends and neighbors and suddenly found themselves facing Cameron's mother, Lady Ravenhurst.

"Good morning, your graces," the older woman greeted the Northingshires, first nodding to North. Then, in a move that shocked them all, she looked right at Helen and smiled sweetly. "What a lovely shade of blue your dress is, Helen. I daresay, once the young ladies see how pretty the color looks on you, they'll all be running to their seamstresses to order the same shade."

Helen, so surprised Lady Ravenhurst was paying her such respect, took a moment to answer. "Th–thank you, your grace," she stammered.

Claudia smiled at the treatment Helen was receiving, but her smile faded when the duchess turned to her with a less-than-friendly expression. "Ah. Lady Claudia."

Claudia took a breath and forced a smile to curve her lips again. "Good morning, your grace," she greeted her brightly, while wondering how Cameron could have been born from such a woman.

With a raised eyebrow and a tight smile, Lady Ravenhurst swept past her. Claudia let out a breath and glanced at Helen. "That was odd, was it not?"

Helen shook her head. "Exceedingly so. I feel like pinching myself to see if I'm dreaming. I can't believe she was so nice to me yet so very rude to you."

"Cameron told me she wasn't happy about my grandfather being one of her former employees."

North guided them to their seats, and Claudia sat on the other side of Helen. "Cameron doesn't seem affected by the news as you had thought. In fact, the way he was looking at you I'd say he likes you very much."

"Shh!" she warned Helen. "Once again you are only imagining things."

"I don't think—" Helen stopped. "There he is! Just in front of us."

Claudia's heart skipped a beat as she looked in the direction Helen was indicating. She saw him and took a moment to appreciate how handsome he looked in his beige and dark brown suit with his white cravat tied at his throat. The colors accented his dark blond hair and warmed his skin tone.

She realized he wasn't alone when he stepped over to sit in the pew.

He was with Aurora Wyndham.

"Oh, dear," Helen whispered—Claudia's exact thoughts. "Isn't that—"

"Aurora Wyndham. They are old friends, I believe," Claudia said. Her tone held no conviction as she watched Aurora whisper something in Cameron's ear. When she saw the smile curve his lips as he turned to say something to her in return, Claudia felt frozen with the realization that for all his teasing about becoming engaged and kissing her, it might be just a game to him.

"I'm sure it's nothing, Claudia," Helen soothed.

"Well, it is none of my business, if it is," she answered, though she felt otherwise. "He's simply a means to get to know my grandfather. That is all."

"But he kissed you! Of course it is your business," Helen said, apparently too loud, for several people looked in their direction.

Including Cameron.

Claudia told herself to look away, but it seemed an impossible task when he sent her a smile which seemed to hold some secret meaning. The moment was broken when he turned back around.

"Oh! I don't believe he was looking at Lady Aurora quite

the way he just gazed at you," Helen said, her voice taking on a dreamy quality. "It fairly took my breath away, and I can only imagine how it made you feel."

Claudia was glad the music started so she didn't have to answer Helen. In truth she didn't know what his smile meant or how she felt about it.

As she stood she determined not to focus on his broad back or the way his hair curled over his collar. Instead she began to sing words of God's grace and prayed He would clear her confusion over her feelings for Cameron.

nine

The next morning Cameron waited by the shelter for Claudia and the Northingshires' arrival and wondered what her reaction would be to him today. When he'd turned and seen her in church, he'd cringed inside at being caught sitting next to Aurora. It was something he hadn't been able to avoid as he entered the church and she had quickly walked up to greet him. If only he'd noticed Claudia first, he could have told his childhood friend that he was with her and the Northingshires. But when he locked gazes with Claudia he'd felt such a strong feeling pass between them, as if everything was all right as long as she was near him. He didn't miss, however, the question in her eyes, and Cameron knew she didn't understand why he was sitting by Aurora.

Cameron let out a weary breath and leaned on the railing of the shelter steps. He had spoken to many of his acquaintances, many who would gladly marry Aurora, if only for the dowry she brought with her, but she refused to accept any of their suits. He tried to reason with her after the service, but she had excuses for every man about why she couldn't marry them. Time was running out for her, and when he reminded her that any man was better than the old Lord Carmichael, she simply smiled and reminded him of his promise to marry her if she couldn't find anyone else.

He sensed a growing worry in his heart over his rash promise. He kept telling himself Aurora felt only friendship and casual affection for him. But another part of him wondered if she hadn't planned to marry him all along.

He quickly shook his head and prayed God would work out

the situation. He was going to be spending the day with the woman he truly wanted to marry. Not even worry over Aurora could muddle his day.

Finally he saw them riding up in North's open conveyance. The duke was driving himself, and Cameron knew it was to bring as little attention to them as possible. The ladies, he was glad to see, were dressed simply and plainly so as not to intimidate the women of the shelter.

Cameron did, however, feel momentarily disappointed he would have to share his time among the three of them instead of with Claudia alone.

"Kinclary!" North greeted him after he helped the ladies from the buggy and then secured the horses to a post. "Are you ready to put us to work?"

Cameron grinned as he shook the duke's hand. "Indeed. There is always something to be done here."

Cameron greeted Helen and then Claudia. "My lady, I don't know how much of George you'll see today, for he is out buying supplies this morning."

Claudia smiled, and he was pleased to see she didn't seem to be upset with him. "I am here to do the Lord's work as much as I'm here for my grandfather, my lord. I just hope no one recognizes me from the other afternoon."

"Trust me, Claudia—when I saw you in my wife's bedroom dressed as you were, I did not recognize you at all!" North cut in, turning to Cameron. "Do you know I came very close to picking her up and throwing her out of the window?"

Cameron laughed as he clapped North on the shoulder and directed him to walk up the steps with him. "Is it because she is American that she does these outlandish things?"

"I beg your pardon!" Claudia blurted out behind Cameron, but North didn't acknowledge her comment.

"It could very well be. You would not believe the things I saw while I lived in Louisiana. I actually saw an Indian kill an alligator using only his knife."

"Unbelievable!" Cameron exclaimed. He'd only seen pictures of such creatures. "And was this Indian civilized, or did he live in the wild like stories I've read?"

"Indeed, he tried to make me believe he wanted to relieve me of my scalp the first time I met him."

"He's talking about Sam," he heard Helen telling Claudia as they entered the building.

Cameron turned to catch Claudia and Helen laughing, as if they shared a funny secret. "Did you know Sam the Indian, Claudia?" he asked her, conjuring up a vision of a tall scantily clad warrior with feathers on his head.

"I've known Sam since we were children. He once offered my father two horses in exchange for my hand. But Helen told me he offered three for her." She gave Helen a mock frown. "I'm quite jealous he liked you better."

Cameron scowled at the two of them. "Gentlemen break their backs trying to woo you ladies with all sorts of gallant and knightly behavior, and then an Indian tries to barter horses for your hand and you become dewy-eyed."

North folded his arms and gave his wife a shrewd look. "Don't let them fool you, Kinclary. Helen gave Sam quite the setting down for his offer and then proceeded to bore him on the rudiments on gentlemanly behavior." He shook his head. "And you notice that Claudia is now living thousands of miles away from him and still unmarried."

All four of them shared a laugh before Cameron got their tour underway. He motioned to the expanse of the large room with his arms. "This is the main room where they stay during the day. They eat and have various lessons here also. Which is what they are doing now." Cameron proudly pointed out the various groups that were learning different tasks from sewing to speaking correctly.

"Servants are always in great demand, but most learn their

craft from their parents and their parents before them. It's my hope I can give these ladies the skills to be ladies' maids, cooks, and even seamstresses," Cameron explained, his voice growing more excited as he spoke. It was hard to put a damper on his enthusiasm because this ministry was so important to him. He truly felt he was doing something that would please Christ.

"I must say, Kinclary, you are fulfilling a need that no one has dared to begin touching," North told him with awe in his voice. "What of spiritual help? Do you have someone to pray with them and help them grow closer to God?"

"Some of the area vicars do come by, but with their own churches to run it is hard for them to come regularly."

North smiled at him. "Then I can tell you God has truly put us together, for I have prayed for an opportunity to minister as I did in Louisiana. If you would not mind, we can hold morning Bible studies and be a comfort to any of the women who need to talk to someone."

As North spoke to him, Cameron felt humbled as he saw God's plan expanding into something even greater than he'd imagined. "That would be wonderful," Cameron told him. "George and I have done most of the work on our own, so it will be a great help to have you here."

From there Cameron showed them the large kitchen and the few employees who worked for him; then he took them to the sleeping quarters, as well as to the classroom where the children gathered around an older woman learning numbers.

Once they ventured back into the main room, Cameron introduced them to some of the women who stayed at the shelter. He was happy to see Claudia greet them warmly without an air of self-importance.

When one of the women greeted her in French, she answered her in the same tongue, sounding as if she were a native of France. Cameron realized he must have let his amazement show because when she looked over at him she grinned and explained,

"Most of South Louisiana is French. My mammy spoke nothing but that language to me as a child."

"Mammy?" Cameron queried, wondering if it was what she called her mother.

"She was the slave woman who took care of me as a child. She'd been born and raised on a Creole plantation until my father purchased her right after my birth."

Cameron was wholeheartedly against any man owning another, no matter how superior they felt they were. But he didn't want Claudia to think he was passing judgment on her, so he treaded carefully. "Your father owns many slaves on his plantation?"

A distressed look fell over her pretty features. "Yes, but when I was old enough to understand what owning slaves meant, I knew it wasn't right. My father was good to his slaves and even freed some of them. But it still did not make it right."

He should have known she felt the same way he did. Hadn't she proved it over and over?

"Kinclary, if you don't mind, we're going to step over here and speak with Mrs. Brantley," North said to him, pulling Cameron's gaze from Claudia. He saw North and Helen standing by a woman who'd come in only the night before. The poor woman had not stopped weeping since she arrived.

"Of course! Please feel free to do whatever you think needs to be done," he said to North.

"Cameron," Claudia spoke his name softly, and he turned back to her. "On the plantation my father gave me permission to teach the children how to read and write. I had to do it in secret because most slave owners forbid such a thing, but I learned a great deal about children. I noticed you only have one teacher for all those children." She paused as if gathering courage. "Perhaps I can take the younger ones, while the other teacher takes the older ones."

Cameron's heart blossomed even more. . .

. . .and he found himself falling more and more in love with her.

"Is there anything Lady Claudia cannot do?" he teased.

She winced and looked away. She seemed so forlorn about what she was about to admit to him, he wondered how bad it could be.

"I can't sing," she said as she brought her gaze back to his. She actually seemed upset by the admission. "I wanted to learn—my father even brought in a voice teacher from New Orleans—but the man said it was too painful to listen to me."

Cameron thought the whole story was hilarious, and though he tried to keep his expression blank, his mirth must have shown through. "I'm sure it's not"—he cleared his throat— "that bad!"

She narrowed her gaze at him. "Are you laughing at me? I'm pouring my heart out to you about my deepest failure, and you think it's funny?" she said in a low, strained voice so as not to draw attention to them.

"No! I—" He couldn't think of how to answer without hurting her, so he took her arm and directed her down the hall. "Let's get you settled into the classroom, eh?"

"You're trying to avoid the subject!" she exclaimed but allowed him to lead her.

"Yes, I am."

"And I suppose you sing splendidly!"

"I'm afraid so," he admitted. He was often asked to share his talent at dinner parties and gatherings. "I've even been known to bring a tear to someone's eye."

She let out a sharp breath. "I know you make me want to cry. *Often*."

He could hold back no longer. He let out a booming laugh as he opened the door to the classroom.

❧

It was hard for Claudia not to join in on his laughter. She was beginning to enjoy their playful sparring, and she wondered if they did become betrothed and married, would he always want to tease her and make her laugh.

What fun that would be.

"Mrs. Owen, this is Claudia Baumgartner," Cameron said when the plump older woman stood. Claudia noticed he'd left off her title, and for that she was grateful. "Mrs. Owen was once my governess before I was sent to Eton. Now that she is retired, she graciously donates her days to teaching our children."

He explained to Mrs. Owen that Claudia could help with the teaching.

Mrs. Owen smiled warmly. "That sounds like an excellent idea. It would be a great help to have you here. Let me introduce you to the children, and tomorrow we can see which child can go in each class."

Claudia greeted each one and was soon sitting with them, helping them write their letters or read a certain word. She didn't know how much time had passed, but when she looked about the room, she half expected Cameron to be gone.

But he wasn't.

He was still leaning against the doorframe, staring at her with a gentle smile on his face. In fact, he had such intense emotion in his eyes that Claudia wanted to jump up and throw herself in his arms.

She had seen a similar look on her father's face as he gazed at her mother when he thought they were alone. Could Cameron be falling in love with her?

It was a heady thought, but one she couldn't help hoping was true.

He finally ended the moment when he gave her a brief wave and left her to the children.

With an excitement bubbling in her chest, Claudia turned back to the student she'd been helping and prayed the time would go by quickly.

After a couple of hours the noonday bell rang out. Both women closed their books and lined up the children.

Claudia allowed Mrs. Owen to lead them out while she brought up the rear. Her path was blocked, though, when a man suddenly turned into the hallway and bumped into her.

"Oh!" She reached out to steady the boxes he was balancing.

"I do apologize. I. . ." His voice faded when their gazes met and each recognized the other.

"Hello." Claudia studied the face of her grandfather Canterbury for the first time and realized she had the same blue eyes as he did.

"Pardon me, my lady." He lowered his gaze at once and began to walk around her.

"But—" She started to protest his cool behavior, but Cameron stepped into the narrow hallway then.

"Ah! George!" His gaze went from George to Claudia. "I didn't know you were back."

"Yes, my lord." He turned his head slightly while keeping his back to them. "I'll just put these away now."

"Wait, Mr. Canterbury! If you could spare me only a bit of your time—," Claudia pleaded and turned to follow him.

But as soon as he entered the storeroom at the end of the hall, he slammed the door behind him. Claudia stood and stared at the wooden door, stunned he would be so rude to her.

Hurt and confusion squeezed at her heart, and at first she felt like weeping. But she was never one to cry overmuch since her stubborn determination usually triumphed over the tears. Taking a deep breath she raised her hand to knock on the door but was stopped before she could make contact.

"Give him some time," Cameron whispered in her ear, lowering her hand.

"But I need to tell him how much I want to get to know him. It's important," she pleaded. She felt comforted, though, as his other hand came to rest on her shoulder.

"I know, Claudia. But his pride and sense of honor are mixed up in this somehow. And sometimes that is all a man has to keep him going," Cameron explained. He turned her around to face him then and gently caressed her cheek. "Why don't you go on into the dining area while I have a word with him? I may not be able to change his mind today, but it may help soften him a bit."

Claudia looked up at him and marveled at how safe and cherished he made her feel. "Thank you, Cameron."

He grinned. "You're welcome, my lady," he said properly, but the low tone in his voice made his words sound more like an endearment.

He let himself into the storeroom and shut the door behind him. Claudia looked around to see if anyone was about, then pressed her ear to the door.

ten

Cameron's smile disappeared the moment he stepped into the storeroom and began looking around for George among the tall shelving. He'd excused George's actions to Claudia, but in truth Cameron was very angry about his butler's behavior.

He finally found the older man sitting on a crate in the last row with his head buried in his hands. His anger faded the moment George lifted his head, and he saw the misery in his eyes.

"I'm sorry, my lord. I know my behavior was inexcusable."

Cameron pulled up another crate and sat across from him. "Tell me what happened," he said kindly.

"She has the features of her mother," he told Cameron, his voice shaky. "I noticed the first night you brought her to your house, after she'd been injured. I guess some part of me knew who she was, but I wouldn't let myself believe it."

Cameron thought back to the night and the way they both looked at each other. "She told me that night that you seemed familiar to her. Family ties are often stronger than we'd like to admit."

George stared down at his hands. "But some have to be broken anyway."

"Not this tie, George. You don't seem to understand—Claudia is not going to rest until you speak with her. You may be stubborn, but she is even more so."

"Are you ordering me to speak with her, my lord?" he asked stiffly, still looking down.

"Of course not, George! I'm just asking you to consider it."

Cameron watched the older man wring his hands. "I'll think on it, my lord," he said finally.

"Thank you, George." He stood to go to the dining area.

"She's important to you, is she?" George asked.

Cameron turned and saw the concern in the old man's eyes. He may not want to speak to his granddaughter, but it didn't mean he didn't care for her. "Yes, she is. Very important."

George simply nodded and stared back down at his hands again, and Cameron left to join the others.

When he reached the main room where everyone was eating, he couldn't find Claudia. His searching gaze met North's eyes, and he stood and crossed the room to Cameron.

"She's outside sitting on the pier," North told him, without his asking.

Cameron smiled sheepishly and clapped North on the shoulder. "Thank you."

As he stepped outside, he spied Claudia standing on the shelter's private pier, which overlooked the Thames. Part of her beautiful dark hair had come loose in the wind and was blowing about her bare neck.

"You're not contemplating jumping in, are you?" he teased, hoping to lighten her gloomy mood. "I'm afraid the smells alone would do you in before the undercurrent could."

She glanced over and tried to smile at his words but only managed a grimace. "I confess I tried to eavesdrop at the door but was unable to hear your conversation." She kept her gaze focused on the water.

Cameron looked up at the sky as he attempted to hide his grin. "Well, I would have expected no less from the woman who befriends pirates and alligator hunters."

This time her small smile was genuine as she peeked at him from the corner of her eye. "Do not keep me in suspense. What did my obstinate grandfather have to say?"

"He says you look very much like your mother, and I believe that looking at you makes him miss her." He bent down and picked up a stick at his feet. He broke off pieces and threw them into the river. "He says he will consider speaking with you, but you must give him time to get used to having you here."

"That's wonderful!" she cried, turning to him with her arms held wide. "When? When will he meet with me?"

Cameron threw the rest of the sticks in the river and, after dusting his hands together, reached and took her hands into his own. "Give him time, Claudia. As he sees you day after day, it will be natural for you to get to know one another slowly."

"But that sounds like an eternity. I want him to acknowledge me now!"

He tucked one of her hands into his arm and led her to an old bench. "Could God be showing you something else in your work here? Patience, perhaps?"

She sat beside him and smoothed her skirts, avoiding his gaze. "I suppose you *could* be right."

Cameron chuckled as he leaned back on the bench, turning slightly toward her. "God has taught me all sorts of needed lessons since I've started the shelter. So you are not alone." He thought of the conversation he had when he visited the family castle. "I learned a valuable one about my father just this week. He's much more aware of my life than I thought."

Claudia glanced at him. "You know, I don't know much about your family. Tell me about them."

His family was quite the odd lot, and he had to think about where he should begin. "Well, you've already met my mother," Cameron said dryly.

Claudia nodded, giggling. "Yes, and she gave me quite the direct cut at church yesterday." He winced.

"Yes, well, let's quickly move on to my father," he said with mock anxiousness, and she laughed again. "My father fancies himself quite a hunter, and though he can't see more than three feet in front of him, he frightens all the poor birds of our shire with his bad shooting. I think he hunts mainly to stay out of the path of my younger sister Lucy. He simply does not know how to handle her."

Claudia nodded. "She sounds a lot like my sister, Josie."

"Katherine has always been the calm, reasonable one, so when Lucy came along he wasn't prepared for her mischief-making ways."

"I'll bet you are a wonderful big brother to your sisters," Claudia said as she looked at him.

He grinned. "If you don't count the time I tried to engage Katherine's husband, who was then her fiancé, in a duel, then I suppose they might say I'm a good brother."

As she smiled at him, he couldn't help but reach up and smooth a stray hair from her face then let his hand linger on her cheek. "You are very beautiful, Claudia," he said softly.

"And you are getting off the subject," she answered him, though she didn't push his hand away.

"Do you realize we have not argued once this whole day?"

"It's an absolute miracle."

"I think it is because you are beginning to like me."

Claudia rolled her eyes and pushed his hand away. "No, it is because you were finally behaving yourself, but apparently you can last only a few hours."

Cameron laughed and stood up, holding his hand out to her. "Come then. Let's go in before you feel the urge to kiss me. I have my reputation at stake, you know."

Claudia ignored his hand and stood on her own, pursing her lips sternly to hide her smile. "You, sir, are a. . .a. . ."

"Cad? Rogue?" he supplied.

"Rascal!" she announced, looking pleased with herself.

He walked her to the door and before opening it said, "But a very lovable rascal, am I not?"

She groaned and covered her face with her hands. He took her hands from her face, kissed them both, and, before she could react, opened the door to the shelter.

❧

The afternoon passed quickly for Claudia as she and Helen finished off the day by playing a game of hide-and-seek with the children. The men were busy bringing in more donated supplies and placing them in the storeroom.

Though she had fun interacting with the children, Claudia's mind kept returning to her conversation with Cameron on the pier. A change in their relationship seemed to have occurred during those few moments; a realization of sorts had come over her, ringing deep in her heart.

She was falling in love with Cameron Montbatten.

Claudia had always thought it would be different when she met the man she wanted to marry. She imagined the gentleman seeking her out at every ball; then after five or six such gatherings the young man would go to her grandfather and ask for her hand in marriage. After that they would go on chaperoned outings to the theater or perhaps a picnic. The wedding would follow after a couple of months, and Claudia and her husband would live happily ever after.

Neat and tidy.

But from the beginning her relationship with Cameron had been like sailing on a ship in rocky waters. She was happy one minute and upset the next. Sometimes she thought Cameron really liked her, and yet at other times she wasn't certain of him at all.

She still did not know how Aurora fit into his life. He never talked about her—never explained why he was sitting by her in church. He had spoken of her being his childhood friend, but didn't friends like that often grow up and marry?

Why couldn't she be certain? Would he go to her grandfather soon and declare his intentions? Would he declare them to *her*?

Claudia stopped a moment to bend down and tie a little girl's shoe. While she did so, the child pulled off the white silk ribbon that had been pinned to Claudia's hair. Knowing her hair was in ruins anyway, Claudia smiled as she took the ribbon and pinned it into the girl's soft blond locks.

She didn't quite expect the little girl to throw her arms around her neck and thank her with so much fervor. One might have thought Claudia had given her a brand-new doll, instead of a piece of silk.

Tears filled her eyes as the child ran back to her mother, proudly showing off her new bow. She was reaching up to dash away the tears when she saw Cameron standing by the doorway, staring at her with eyes filled with an unfathomable emotion.

Embarrassed by her display of emotion, she stood and busily brushed her skirts, hoping he'd just walk past her.

But Cameron, she knew, had a mind of his own.

"I believe you are the only woman I've ever known to stay dry-eyed after being accosted yet cry when a little girl thanks you for a trinket," he observed, walking up to her.

She felt under her eyes to make sure they weren't wet. "I was hoping you didn't notice that. I usually never cry and—"

He stopped her with his hand on her arm. "I wouldn't have missed it for the world, my lady."

He smiled at her then strolled down the hall where the other men were. She glanced down at her arm and saw she still had goose bumps from the adoring look he'd flashed in her direction.

"Oh, my!" Helen said, startling Claudia.

"Uh. . .where did you come from?" she asked her friend as nonchalantly as she could manage. "I was about to come and find you."

"Of course you were," she said, smiling. "And I suppose the amorous exchange I just witnessed between you and Cameron was a conversation about the weather."

Claudia opened her mouth to refute what Helen was

implying, but she was eager to confide in someone. "Actually I don't know what happened. I fear I am falling in love with him, but I am uncertain if he feels the same for me."

Helen shook her head. "Claudia, it is obvious Lord Kinclary is head over heels in love with you. He looks at you every time he enters the room."

"He does?"

"Yes, and did you know he asked North to make sure we took you home every day? He doesn't want you going to our home and then walking home by yourself."

Claudia considered her words for a moment. "But, Helen, shouldn't he tell me of his feelings or perhaps go to my grandfather and state his intentions?"

Helen nodded. "Yes, but give him time, Claudia. With the shelter on his mind and George on yours, he might want to take things slow. I'm sure he will not be able to wait long."

Claudia was not convinced but decided there was no use worrying about it either. "I hope you're right. It's so difficult having these feelings and not hearing them reciprocated from the man you love."

Helen nodded and smiled. "I went through the same thing with North. I loved him for years, even though everyone around me told me such a match could never be." She patted Claudia on the shoulder. "Just keep believing God has it all under control. If you are meant to be married, then God will make it so."

Hearing her words made Claudia feel more confident. She had been praying for God's guidance in her life, and He had led her to the shelter. It also seemed He had led her straight into the path of the Earl of Kinclary. Of course God would give her the answers she needed.

"There is one thing, though," Helen spoke again. Claudia did not like the hesitation in her friend's voice. "I spoke with Katherine, Cameron's sister, yesterday. She mentioned something about Aurora Wyndham and a rumor that Aurora's father has given her an ultimatum to find a husband or else he'll marry her off to old Lord Carmichael."

Claudia frowned. "Hasn't he already been married four times?"

"Yes, and she said Aurora has been pleading with Cameron to help her find a husband."

Suddenly Claudia felt lighter. "This is why he's been talking to her so much. He's helping her make a match!"

Helen wasn't smiling. "Yes, but I don't know if I trust Aurora, and neither does Katherine. She told me Aurora was very good at manipulating people, and Katherine fears she's using this only to get Cameron to marry her."

The light feeling left and was replaced by a sinking one. "Perhaps Cameron has feelings for Aurora, too," she said faintly, hating the words as she spoke them.

"God will sort it out," Helen told her again more firmly.

"Of course He will," she answered, then prayed He would "sort it out" in her favor.

eleven

"Lady Claudia! Please pay attention!" Mr. Loveless ordered in an irritating nasal tone, tapping the board with his piece of chalk. He so startled Claudia out of her daydreaming state that her elbow slid off her desk and hit her funny bone.

Cradling her elbow and grimacing with pain, she responded to him, not even trying to mask her annoyance. "I've told you, Mr. Loveless—I know rules of proper address. *Must* we keep going through it?"

He pinched his thin lips together, pushing his wire spectacles higher on his long nose. "I have been hired by his grace because he believes you to be ignorant on the subject of peerage, Lady Claudia, but for that to be accomplished I must have your cooperation!" He glared at her, then reached in his pocket and drew out his gold watch, snapping it open with a flick of his thumb. "Since it is the noon hour I shall allow you to break for lunch."

Claudia blew out a relieved breath and started to rise from her seat. "*However*," he said, and she slumped back down, "I suggest you carry your notes with you and study them as you eat. We shall discuss them when you return at one o'clock sharp."

Claudia didn't move in case he had anything else to add. But when he sat at his desk and started to draw food out of his bag, she stood and all but ran from the room.

It had been like this for two days—ever since her grandfather found out she had addressed Baron Willetton as "sir" and not "my lord" at one of the balls she'd attended. He'd immediately sent out for Mr. Loveless, a tutor who specialized in the English Peerage, a directory of all the titled noble men and women of England. Then she'd been ordered to her old classroom and treated as if she were twelve instead of twenty!

The worst part of this whole debacle was that she'd not been able to go back to the shelter since the first day. The only thing her grandfather would allow her to do was send a note to Helen and read her reply.

Helen had assured her she would let Cameron know why she wasn't coming to the shelter and that she and North would continue to work without her.

The irony of this lesson her grandfather thought he was teaching her was that she already knew how to address the nobility. In fact she could practically name all those who served in the House of Lords, their lesser titles, and what son would inherit them. She'd misspoken the baron's title but only because someone had introduced him as a baronet, who did use the title of "sir."

Instead of going to the dining room where she usually had lunch with her aunt, she went to her room to ask that her food be brought up. She was pleasantly surprised when she found Helen waiting for her there.

"Helen!" She walked to the settee where her friend sat reading one of her books. "What are you doing here?"

Helen tossed the book on the seat and jumped up to meet Claudia. "I've come to rescue you!"

Claudia shook her head. "How will you accomplish this? Grandfather has been adamant that I spend at least a week being tutored."

"I told him I need you to help me plan a ball."

Claudia looked at Helen for a moment. "A ball? I didn't know you were planning a ball."

Helen giggled. "Well, I wasn't until today."

Claudia shook her head. "But I can't believe this alone would convince him."

"Well," Helen drew out as if she were teasing her with a great secret, "it didn't at first. But when I told him the prince regent would be there and I needed your opinion on choosing invitations and such, he readily agreed."

Claudia giggled along with her friend. "You are quite a planner, aren't you? But how did you manage to get the prince to agree?"

"North is a distant cousin, as you know, but even that didn't sway him until we mentioned *you* were helping us put on the ball."

Claudia groaned. "It is only because he wants to hear more of my stories about Louisiana," she grumbled. "But I have told him all I know."

Helen smiled confidently and patted her arm. "Then retell them. I'm sure he won't mind hearing them again."

Claudia sighed. "I must confess I know nothing of planning a ball other than what my tutors have taught me."

Helen shrugged. "Neither do I. North does, though, so we'll follow his lead."

Claudia was about to change the subject and ask how Cameron was doing when Helen stepped around her and opened up her wardrobe.

"What are you doing?" Claudia asked curiously. She walked over to watch Helen sifting through her dresses.

"Trying to find the perfect gown." Helen paused and studied a silk dress in a particular shade of deep blue. "No, this doesn't set the right tone," she murmured and kept sorting through the others.

"The right tone for what?" Claudia asked, peeking over Helen's shoulder. The blue dress wasn't one of her favorites either.

"Hmm?" She glanced back. "Oh! The theatre, dear. North has a box at Covent Gardens." She pulled out a beautiful cream-colored silk with a lace overlay. It had a matching pelisse dyed one shade darker in a sort of beige hue. "Perfect!" she exclaimed, admiring the seed pearls sewn in the trim of the neckline and cap sleeves.

"The theatre? I thought we were planning a ball?" Claudia figured she must have been cooped up in the classroom too long, for she was having trouble following Helen's plans.

Helen pulled the dress from the wardrobe and laid it out on Claudia's bed. She then pulled the cord, which called Claudia's lady's maid, Cummings. "Well, since Lord Moreland seemed so agreeable about the ball, I thought I'd see if he would let you attend the theatre with us tonight. He readily agreed, much to my surprise, citing that it might be an excellent opportunity for the eligible young men of London to see you."

Claudia groaned, pressing her hand to her forehead. "Does he think of nothing else?"

Helen laughed. "Does any father or grandfather of the ton?"

At that moment Cummings came in, and Helen instructed her to pack her dress and have it sent to Northingshire Manor. Then, after Claudia dressed to leave the house, they made their way down to Helen's waiting carriage.

"What is playing at the theatre by the way?" Claudia asked as they climbed in and got settled comfortably.

Helen shrugged with a giggle. "I don't know. They all seem the same to me. An opera in which the characters sing their conversations instead of speaking them and then someone usually dies at the end."

Claudia laughed then lapsed into silence trying to think of a casual way to bring up the subject of Cameron.

"So," she began, trying to appear blasé as she examined her nails, "how are the women and children at the shelter?"

Helen studied her. "Well, two new women came in, and one had a set of twins who were very cute. And let's see. . ." She paused and tapped on her chin. "Oh, yes! Young Johnny Smith lost one of his front teeth. It was quite a gruesome sight since he pulled it out himself while standing in front of me. But I managed to bring him to his mother before I lost the contents of my stomach. Then. . ." She paused again, and Claudia could take no more.

"Could you please just tell me how Cameron is, and has he asked about me?" she demanded, throwing her hands up in exasperation.

Helen's eyes widened. "But you didn't ask about Cameron. You asked about the wom—"

"I know what I asked, Helen! And I know you're teasing me horribly." She narrowed her eyes, and Helen giggled.

"All right! If you must know, Lord Kinclary has been asking constantly about you, prying information from me at every opportunity. He now knows your entire life story—at least all I'm aware of. Unfortunately most of my information came from your little sister, so it's not completely accurate."

Claudia covered her cheeks and groaned. "I'm almost afraid to ask what Josie told you. Did he. . .uh. . .give any hint of his feelings toward me?"

Helen's eyes widened. "You must be joking! The man mentions you in every conversation. And though he hasn't come right out and declared his intentions toward you, it's apparent to all that he thinks fondly of you."

Claudia clasped her hands to her chest and sighed. "I can't wait to see him. Do you think we might have time to go to the shelter tomorrow? I know we must plan the ball, but surely we have an hour or two to spare."

Helen nodded. "I'm sure it can be arranged." She paused as the carriage rattled to a stop. "Oh, here we are! Now let's go and get you ready for tonight."

Claudia frowned and, scampering out of the carriage, ran to keep up with her. "Now? It's only noon."

"Come on! It takes a lot of time to make ourselves beautiful for a night out."

Claudia could think of a hundred things more fun to do

than spend time beautifying herself. She wasn't much in the mood to go to the theatre, but she knew Helen was trying to cheer her up.

And she did feel better once she, Helen, and North finally arrived and were taken to their private box. Claudia still didn't understand why Helen had taken such pains to dress her.

All afternoon she had been bathed and powdered while Helen fussed with her lady's maid over every detail of Claudia's dress. Then, in what usually took less than an hour to accomplish, Helen had her maid style Claudia's straight hair into an array of curls, which were pinned loosely at the crown and fell in a bunch over her shoulder. She prayed she wouldn't find the whole lot of her hair singed from spending so much time twisted in the curling tongs.

"Why don't you sit in the front seat, and North and I will sit behind you?" Helen waved her hand toward the velvet chair in the box.

Feeling slightly like the unwanted third in their party, Claudia sighed and took her seat then began to skim over the small program booklet they'd been handed upon their arrival. She recognized a few names on the actors' list and was trying to place what other play a certain actor had been in when she felt a hand on her shoulder.

"Helen," she said, without glancing back, "I can't place where I've heard this person's name before. Do you know—"

She looked up then and was shocked to see Cameron slipping into the chair next to her. Now Helen's odd behavior was finally making sense.

She turned around in her chair, with her back to Cameron, and sent her friend a brilliant smile. Her face was serene and calm, though, when she turned back to the handsome man beside her and greeted him.

❧

Claudia's soft smile sent a jolt straight to his heart while he gazed at her in the dim light of the theatre. Her dark hair framed her creamy skin and dusty pink cheeks, and her eyes seemed to glisten like the sea. He'd missed her so much in those last two days that one might think they'd been separated a year, the way his palms were sweating and his heart beating so madly.

He sat down and watched her hesitate. But before he could say anything she took a breath. . .and said his name.

"Good evening, Cameron," her voice whispered in what sounded like a caress. Did he imagine it, or was there much feeling in the way she spoke his name?

He knew certain gossipers would be watching them as much as they watched the stage, so he wanted to be above reproach from their speculative stares.

But he didn't realize how much his love for her had flourished in such a short time and how hearing his name uttered by her sweet lips would affect him.

It was the most natural thing in the world to reach for her gloved hand and press a kiss to it. "How very lovely you are tonight, Claudia." His voice sounded hoarse even to his own ears.

"*Lord Kinclary.*" Helen's fretful tone caused them both to turn to her. "We do not want to bring attention to ourselves!"

Cameron winced as he skimmed the patrons' faces below them and caught furtive glances being thrown their way.

"We shall be the talk of all London tomorrow." Claudia moaned and scrambled to untie her fan, which was attached to her purse, and snap it out to partly cover her face.

Cameron couldn't help but grin at the pointless effort. "I don't think that will help, Claude. Everyone here knows who you are."

He heard a strange sound behind him, and when he looked back, he saw that it was North doing a poor job of holding back a chuckle. Helen sighed and nudged him with her elbow.

"Yes, thanks to you and your inability to *not* kiss me every time we meet." She stopped and frowned, lowering the fan to her lap. "Did you just call me *Claude*?"

Cameron grinned. "Yes, it slipped out, but now that it's out there I believe it suits you."

He watched her shake her head and take another glimpse at the audience below. "Well, I don't like it. Call me something else!"

He peeked down with her and was glad to see many had lost interest in them. "Such as what? Darling? Sweetheart?"

She glared at him. "You are behaving very badly tonight. If you keep smiling at me like that, people might get the wrong idea."

Or they might get the right one, Cameron thought but decided against speaking it aloud.

"As entertaining as both of you are, perhaps we should direct our attention to the stage so the actors won't get their feelings hurt when they find everyone watching you instead of them!" North whispered, his voice full of mirth.

Cameron looked at the stage and saw that, indeed, the curtains were open and the music had just begun.

He glanced at Claudia, and they both exchanged sheepish grins before turning their attention to the play.

Cameron could not have told anyone what the play was about, for he spent most of his time either thinking about Claudia and their relationship or observing her face. He loved how her emotions would change with the play from happy to sad and even to tears.

He loved many things about Claudia. The obvious ones— her kindness, her sense of humor, her cheerfulness, and, most of all, her love for God. But he also liked the little things—the way she was so quick to catch him when he teased her, the way she would lift her finely arched brow whenever she was trying hard not to laugh, and so many more.

He loved her—plain and simple.

In fact, if it hadn't been for his rash promise to Aurora, he'd have already declared himself and spoken with Claudia's grandfather about marriage.

But the promise was there, hanging like an albatross around his neck. Cameron knew he must resolve the issue before he could ask Claudia to marry him. He didn't want there to be any obstacles standing in their path while they prepared to start their lives together.

As the curtain finally fell, he heard sniffles and looked to see both Claudia and Helen drying their tears.

"Weren't the music and the characters so moving?" Claudia asked him.

Cameron took a moment to study her dewy eyes and tear-stained cheeks. She was even beautiful when she cried. "I know I was moved," he answered, giving Claudia a loving, caressing smile.

He heard the same noise he'd heard earlier from North and glanced back in time to see Helen nudging him again. North ignored the nudge. "What character moved you the most, Kinclary?" he asked, his voice slightly choked.

"No, please, North. I insist you give us your assessment first," his wife countered with her arms folded.

"You three are acting very strange," Claudia chimed in, glancing back and forth between the three of them.

Cameron thought this might be a good time to change the subject. "Shall we go?"

"Capital idea!" North seconded, tucking his wife's arm into his and directing her out of the box.

Cameron held out his arm to Claudia and smiled as he suddenly remembered a name he'd heard from the play. "Roger!"

She shook her head. "I beg your pardon?"

"Roger," he said again. "I believe the character Roger was the most memorable of the play."

He knew he had said the wrong thing when she looked at him in astonishment. "Do you mean Roderick?"

Cameron swallowed. "Oh! Ah. . .yes. That's it. Sorry." He picked up her hand and folded it into his arm. "You know, we'd better hurry and catch up with them. We could lose them in the crowd."

He pulled her out of the box and into the hallway. "So what did you like about Roderick?" she persisted, much to his dismay, as they walked down the stairway.

Where was a good diversion when he needed one? "Hmm. Let's see," he said thoughtfully. Finally he settled on a safe answer. "He was a likeable character."

Apparently it wasn't the safe answer he needed, for she sent him an incredulous stare. "You must be joking. Roderick was the murderer!"

Cameron managed to smile at her, while he hoped this conversation would soon be over. "Of course I'm joking, Claude. Now let's make haste and find Helen and North."

"My name is not Claude!"

Cameron only smiled as he finally spotted their friends and started walking toward them.

twelve

The next morning, Claudia awoke with a jolt when she felt her bed shift from under her. Disoriented, she quickly scrambled to push the hair from her face, only to find Helen bouncing on the side of the bed and grinning at her. "Claudia! Get up, sleepyhead! I've been waiting for an hour to hear the details of what happened with the two of you last night and will simply perish with curiosity if you do not tell me."

Claudia groaned, then slowly sat up in bed. She looked about, confused by her surroundings, until she remembered she'd spent the night at Helen's home. "You are much too cheerful in the morning." She rubbed her eyes and yawned. She saw Helen was dressed in a lilac gown, which made her blue eyes seem almost violet. Her shiny black hair was pinned up with violets scattered throughout.

"And *you* are a grouch!" She climbed off the bed and crossed the room to a table where a tea service had been laid out.

Claudia wearily pulled her legs over the side of the bed and sat on the edge. "What hour is it?"

Helen handed Claudia a cup of tea then fetched her own. "It is nine in the morning, and you must hurry and dress because we are to be at Kinclary's house at ten."

Claudia's eyes brightened, and suddenly she had more energy. "Cameron? He sent a note?"

Helen glanced at Claudia over her teacup. "Yes, he did, and I must say it's amazing how the man's name can transform your entire mood." Claudia frowned at her, and Helen giggled. "He was inquiring as to whether he could ride to the shelter with us this morning since one of the wheels on his conveyance is being repaired. North sent him word that we'd come around for him at ten."

Claudia was feeling a little more awake, and memories of the previous night began to flood her mind. "I never thanked you for inviting Cameron to the theatre last night. What a lovely surprise it was."

Helen put her hand to her chest. "When he kissed your hand, I sat mesmerized at the way he was looking at you with such feeling."

Claudia cringed. "You along with everyone else. Do you think people are still talking about it?"

"I'm afraid even those who weren't there will be talking about it," Helen told her hesitantly. "It was remarked upon in the *Times* this morning."

Claudia's cup hit the saucer with a clang. "What did they write?" she asked weakly, setting the cup and saucer on her night table.

"Something about wedding bells might be ringing for Lord K and Lady C since they are making no effort to hide their affection for one another in public."

Claudia covered her face. What would the repercussions be when her grandfather read the paper? "This is horrible! Grandfather will get his hopes up that I've finally made a match," she cried. "What will Cameron think? Will he believe I planned such a thing to happen so he'd have to propose?"

Helen put her own cup down and took Claudia's hands. "*He* kissed *you*—remember? If he feels any pressure, then it's his own fault. Besides, the man is quite taken with you, Claudia. He watched you more than he did the play." She smiled. "Which is why he couldn't remember any of the characters!"

Claudia smiled. "I *did* catch him looking at me a few times. And he didn't seem *too* upset when he realized everyone had been watching him kiss my hand."

"He's smitten with you, dear friend. That I am sure of."

Claudia felt a surge of energy go through her at that thought, and she suddenly couldn't wait to see Cameron again. Jumping up, she pulled Helen along with her. "Let's not waste a minute more then. Help me dress!"

Helen called her maid, and in no time at all they were ready, and the three of them were on their way to Cameron's townhouse.

Claudia's stomach was fluttering with excitement as they turned on Cameron's street. It was such a beautiful day to ride in the open carriage, and Claudia was looking forward to sharing the morning with Cameron, sitting close to him, with the fresh spring wind blowing through their hair.

As they drew closer she noticed two people standing in front of his residence. "It looks as if he may have visitors," Claudia observed.

North squinted in the glaring sun and nodded. "I believe one of them is Cameron, from the size of him, and the other is a lady."

Claudia frowned. "Can you tell who it is? Is it his sister?"

"No," replied Helen, "I believe it's—" She stopped before she named the person. Claudia glanced at her.

"What's wrong, Helen?" She looked back at the couple. They were closer now, and Claudia recognized the woman. She could feel her heart sinking. "Oh. . ."

Aurora Wyndham.

"I'm sure it's nothing," Helen assured her.

Claudia thought back to the night before and how loving Cameron was to her. "I'm sure you are right."

But they were standing very close to one another, and Claudia saw that Aurora was holding on to Cameron's arm as if it were the most natural thing to do.

❧

"Aurora, I've no time to speak of this matter again with you." Cameron told her for the second time. He raised his eyes and noticed North's carriage coming toward them. Then he saw Claudia.

And she was looking at him from the carriage with hurt, stricken eyes.

Cameron jerked his gaze back to Aurora and realized how their close stance could be misconstrued. Cameron pulled his arm away and stepped back from her. "Aurora!" he snapped when she tried to grab his arm again. "Please worry me no more today on this issue and be on your way."

She finally backed away, and Cameron glanced up to see that, though the carriage had stopped, its occupants had remained in the vehicle.

Drawing in a calming breath he looked back at Aurora and saw she was whimpering, but in fact no tears were falling from her eyes. He wondered why she was burdening him with this whole engagement fiasco. Then again hadn't she always run to him whenever she was in trouble?

And he had always bailed her out and saved the day. Now if he could just find her a husband, then *he* could handle her instead of Cameron.

The problem was, finding a husband for Aurora seemed to be a nearly impossible task.

"Aurora, I have spoken to five good gentlemen who were willing to take you as a wife. I don't understand why you have rejected every one of them." Cameron tried to hurry the conversation along so he wouldn't keep Claudia waiting.

"Don't you understand, Cam?" she said with another sniff. "My father's estate has dwindled terribly, along with my dowry, because of some bad investments. I didn't reject those gentlemen. They rejected me when I told them I was practically penniless."

Cameron resisted the urge to groan with frustration. The fact that she was wealthy was the only reason his acquaintances were willing to overlook all her bad qualities. Aurora had a reputation for being selfish, vain, and unconcerned about anyone's problems but her own. Without a dowry he didn't know many men who would be willing to take her for a wife.

"Aurora, I'm sure we can figure out something. I—"

"Why don't we just become engaged, Cam?" she interrupted with a pleading pout to her lips. "We can go to my father today, and I won't have this worry to contend with anymore."

He noticed North glancing at his pocket watch and sent him a look of apology. "Aurora, I don't want to become engaged to you. I've told you this. Now my friends are waiting for me, so—"

"Yes, I've heard about Lady Claudia. The ton is all abuzz about your night at the theatre," she said with a sneer. "Don't forget your promise to me, Cam. You may not want to become engaged to me now, but you promised you would if I cannot find someone else to marry me."

"I haven't forgotten, Aurora. Just please try to settle for someone else, for both our sakes." He waved at North to drive up closer. "Now, if you'll excuse me, I have an appointment to keep."

He walked around her and climbed in the carriage then sat by Claudia.

"I'm sorry for the delay. Her visit was not a scheduled one," he apologized as simply as he could without going into detail.

North and Helen told him it was fine and waved away his concern, but Claudia remained quiet beside him. He glanced her way and started to explain more as to why Aurora was there, but she abruptly leaned forward and tapped Helen on the shoulder.

"Helen, I just remembered where I've seen the actor from last night's play. He was at a dinner party thrown by my third cousin Howard, and. . ." Claudia chattered on about the play for several minutes until he could take no more of her ignoring him.

"Claudia, will you please cease your chatter for a moment?" he almost shouted. He hadn't realized how forceful he had sounded until all three occupants of the carriage turned and frowned at him.

                          ❧

Claudia, startled into silence, stared at Cameron with surprise and confusion over his unusual lack of composure. She had known he'd wanted to explain as she chattered on inanely, but she hadn't wanted him to think she'd been affected by the friendly display on his doorstep.

"I apologize for shouting. It's just that I've been trying to explain about what you three saw when you drove up." He glanced between all of them but spoke mainly to Claudia.

"There's no need to explain." Claudia forced herself to smile. "It's none of our business whom you keep company with." Even as she spoke it, she wished she could take it back. She could hear the hurt in her own voice.

She ventured a peek at Cameron, and apparently he could hear it also. "I see," he said slowly. "But are you sure it's not *your* business?" he directed to her ears only.

Perhaps she should have given him the benefit of the doubt, but she was so confused as to why he had not declared his feelings to her. "Quite sure, since we are not betrothed or attached in any way." It was the worst sort of hint to pass to a gentleman, but Claudia was too upset and bewildered to care at this point.

When Cameron didn't comment, she glanced at him again to see his reaction to her words. Finally he sat back on his seat and stared straight ahead. "You're right, of course," he said stiffly.

Claudia looked away to hide her pain. Why couldn't he tell her how he felt? What was stopping him from making known his intentions toward her? Usually, if a gentleman spent even half the time he had with her, it would be understood a betrothal would soon follow. And now, with the ton speculating about them, it puzzled her as to why he would not make a move.

Unless Aurora *did* have some sort of hold on him. Was the story of her father making a marriage demand on her true? Was Cameron helping her find a match, or did he plan to marry Aurora himself?

These questions and many more about Cameron were plaguing her as they arrived at the shelter and she went to her classroom.

The whole morning Claudia kept expecting Cameron to glance in and say hello to her, but he did not. She spied him walking past the open door many times, but he never once looked in.

Fortunately the children were such a joy to teach. She was able for a little while at least to take her mind off Cameron and focus it on something worthwhile.

At last the lunch bell rang out, and both teachers lined up the children and escorted them out into the main room. She glanced around, and, though she saw North and Helen, Cameron was nowhere to be found.

Throughout the noon hour she barely touched her stew. It didn't make sense, though, that she should feel so bad when it was *he* who was caught with another woman in front of his entire neighborhood.

Why was he evading her presence when she had done nothing but tell him the truth? While it was true her attitude had not been exactly civil, he should still be a gentleman about the whole thing and quit hiding like a child.

Fueled by her ire she stood up from the table. "Mrs. Owen, if you'll excuse me for a moment, I have something to take care of."

Mrs. Owen smiled and waved her off. She had to walk by Helen on the way to Cameron's office, and just as she'd feared her friend called out to her.

"Claudia! Where are you going?" Helen asked, her eyes keenly scanning Claudia's expression.

"I'll be right back," Claudia answered evasively, continuing on and ignoring Helen's request for her to return.

Helen had to know something must be done. She didn't want to work at the shelter while he ignored her day in and day out.

Before she could touch the door handle, Cameron's door swung open. Cameron walked out in front of her, nearly knocking her over.

"I do apologize. . . ," he began, grabbing hold of her shoulders, but his words drifted off when he realized it was Claudia. His hands jerked away from her as if she were suddenly on fire, and he stumbled back a step. "If you'll excuse me," he told her, avoiding her gaze, then hurried away from her.

Stunned, she watched him disappear into the main room. Was he running from her?

Perhaps he was, she thought. Why couldn't he even look at her? Had his feelings changed from last night when he'd kissed her hand so gently? It must have to do with his visit with Aurora, but what?

"Excuse me, my lady," she heard a man say to her in a brisk tone. She then noticed her grandfather scooting around her and hurrying into his own office.

She flinched at the sound of his door slamming behind him. He hadn't looked at her either.

What was wrong with the men in her life? Why did they have to drive her to madness as these two seemed to do?

Enough was enough, she thought with renewed determination. She marched up to her grandfather's door and opened it without knocking.

The older man looked up, his eyes wide, a frown creasing his brows. But Claudia didn't care. With a thrust of her chin and a fortified breath, she walked over to his desk.

"Hello, Grandfather," she said as if it were the most natural thing in the world to say. She watched his expression go from disbelief to surprise then to something indiscernible before he turned his head.

"I'm very busy now, so if you could please—"

"Leave?" she supplied for him, her heart aching with every word he spoke. "No. I will not leave until you look me in the eyes and tell me why you don't want to know me." She was thankful her voice didn't break since tears were beginning to sting the backs of her lids.

She thought he was going to ignore her request, but then he turned and looked at her. She could scarcely believe it when she saw tears swimming in the older man's eyes.

Claudia couldn't help herself. She ran around the desk and threw her arms around him. "I knew you had to love me!" Tears of joy fell onto her cheeks and spilled over onto his coat.

"Of course I do, child. That was never the problem." He hugged her to him.

She stepped back to look up into his eyes. "Whatever the problem is, Grandfather, we can deal with it. You are as much my family as Grandfather Moreland is."

His eyes had a sadness about them. "But you will one day be the Marchioness of Moreland and—"

"And you'll still be my grandfather!" she interrupted. "I don't care what the ton thinks of it. I need you in my life, and I think you need me, too."

She looked up at him with eyes full of hope and was thrilled when he reached out and patted her head affectionately. "You are as stubborn as your mother, do you know that?"

She grinned. "I've been told this on many occasions."

He hesitated then asked, "How is my daughter? Is she well?"

Claudia gladly filled him in on how her mother and father were doing in Louisiana. She also told him about her little sister, Josie.

They spoke several more minutes about her mother, and then he changed the subject. "I suppose you and my employer will soon be making an announcement. But it might make things awkward with me as his butler."

Hope rose like spring flowers when she heard his words. "Grandfather, he has made no promises to me. Has he said anything to you that would lead you to believe he means to make an offer for my hand?"

Her grandfather seemed taken aback. "I don't understand, Claudia. I assumed by the time you have spent together that he had made known his intentions." He rubbed his chin thoughtfully. "Has he said anything to you about Aurora?"

Claudia sighed, weary of hearing her name. "She was with him this morning when we arrived to pick him up. They seem very close," she told him.

"Lord Kinclary has always spent a lot of time with her, but I was under the impression he thought of her as a sister. She appears to depend on him more than she should, and for some reason he feels he must help her."

Claudia nodded, feeling a little better by his assurance. "I will confess, Grandfather George, I do love him and wish he would give me some sort of sign that he feels the same." She wanted him to know the true nature of her feelings.

Her grandfather nodded. "By the way he looks at you, Claudia, I do not doubt you will hear that proposal sooner than later."

Claudia smiled at him, then left him to finish her work.

But after she went back to the dining area, she noticed Cameron look her way, then stand. Her heart raced when she thought he was going to come over to her, but she was mistaken.

Cameron merely put away his plate and walked out the front door of the shelter.

thirteen

The two weeks that followed her reunion with her grandfather George were the happiest Claudia had experienced since she'd arrived in England. Though it had been difficult at first to get him to speak easily with her, he grew more and more comfortable every day. He'd even insisted she call him Grandpapa because it was more casual than what she called the marquis.

The rift between her and Cameron had been mended also. It had lasted a couple of days until she swallowed her pride and apologized for snapping at him after seeing him with Aurora. He in turn asked for her forgiveness concerning his own behavior. He went on to explain about Aurora's dilemma with her father and that he was helping her find a husband.

He'd seemed nonchalant about the whole ordeal, but Claudia had the feeling he wasn't telling her everything. And in the days that followed the feeling remained.

It was only compounded by the fact that Cameron still had not stated his intentions toward her.

She had also noticed a reserve about him whenever they were alone together. There were no more kisses, no overt flirting, and even no tucking the strands of her hair back as he'd done before. He was the picture of a perfect gentleman.

What was wrong with him? she wondered with exasperation.

It was almost as if he were biding his time, waiting for something.

But what?

She shouldn't complain, she reminded herself nearly every day. Claudia was the one with whom he talked about his expansion plans for the shelter, and he always said "we" as if he were expecting her to be with him forever. They went to the theatre, walked through the park, and attended church with one another. Every few days the paper would comment on where they were seen and when they would set the wedding date.

Claudia was sure Cameron read the newspaper, but he never remarked on what they wrote.

The only answer she could come up with was that Aurora must have something to do with his seeming reluctance. The rumor about the ton was that she was actively looking for a husband, but any who seemed interested were turned away.

Could she be hoping Cameron would marry her? Was Cameron waiting for Aurora to become engaged before he would make an offer for Claudia's hand? If so, why would he do that—why would it matter?

What hold did Aurora Wyndham have over the man Claudia loved?

"Claudia! Are you going to stare at those flowers all day or give them to Ella to thread through my hair?" Helen asked, snapping Claudia out of her perplexing thoughts. Claudia looked down and realized she'd picked at least ten more flowers from the garden than they could possibly need.

Shading her eyes with her hand, she looked up at Helen, who was leaning out of her window. "Sorry. I got a bit melancholy out here surrounded by all these pink roses," she admitted with a sheepish grin, then made her way to the door.

"Why is this not surprising?" Helen called after her. Claudia ran into the house then and up the stairs to Helen's room.

In the last two weeks Claudia and Helen had worked tirelessly to prepare for the ball. There were flower arrangements to order, silverware and dishware to decide upon, and invitations to post. Then they had to decide on the orchestra and what desserts the prince regent expected to be available.

All very tedious indeed. Yet, as they dressed for the awaited event, Claudia felt a sense of accomplishment and hoped the night would go as anticipated.

The whole Northingshire household, of course, was aflutter with nervous activity. Christina, their friend and now the Countess of Kenswick, had come to help them, and all three were now putting on the last touches of their evening attire.

This was why she'd been down gathering roses for their hair.

"Claudia, you must put on your gown!" Christina scolded the moment she walked into the room. "What were you doing in the garden so long?"

Claudia sighed as she handed over the roses to the maid. "Well, I—"

"She was daydreaming about Cameron again—*this* you can be sure of," Helen cut in teasingly while her maid began styling her hair.

"I want to know why the man is taking so long in declaring his feelings to you, Claudia," Christina said, studying herself critically in the mirror.

Christina was the most vivacious and talkative noblewoman Claudia had come across since she'd been in England. She stood tall, with red, curly hair, and loved to recount her stories of how she met her husband while climbing a tree. She also told tales of the many animals she had doctored and kept as pets, much to her husband's dismay.

Christina was one to come right out and speak whatever was on her mind—as she was at this moment.

"If I were you, I would step up to him and demand he tell me what his intentions are. There would be no more mystery, and you could finally go on with your life."

Helen started to laugh, while Claudia looked at her with unbelief. "I couldn't do that!" she gasped. And then she thought about it. "Could I?"

"No, you could not. Christina, tell her you are only teasing," Helen admonished.

Christina grinned, glancing over her shoulder as her own maid adjusted the bows on her dark green gown. "All right, but it would certainly put him on the spot, wouldn't it?"

Claudia groaned as she held up her arms and allowed her maid to pull her dress over her. "What of Aurora? Have you heard anything about her in connection with Cameron?"

Christina shook her head. "I'm afraid not. She hasn't been seen at any of the balls I've attended, and some have speculated she may have retired to her father's country home in Devon."

There was a knock at the door, which prevented Claudia from speaking her next sentence. Since Christina was the only one fully dressed, she went to answer the door.

She spoke quietly to the servant, then turned back to the room with a note in her hand. With a smile of expectancy she waved the note toward Claudia. "It's for you."

Claudia crossed over to her, though her dress was still unfastened. "Who is it from?" she asked faintly.

Christina handed her the sealed paper. "He didn't say. Open it, open it!" she urged.

Helen, with part of her hair hanging down, ran over to join them. Not a one of them breathed as Claudia opened the note and read it.

"It's from Cameron," she announced breathlessly.

"I knew it!" Christina said. "What does he say?"

Claudia clasped the letter to her chest. "He wants to meet me on the terrace at eight o'clock."

Helen put her arm around her. "That's an hour after the ball has begun. What do you suppose he wants?"

"He wants to ask her to marry him, of course!" Christina answered.

Claudia wanted to believe it, but she was too afraid to. "Let's not get excited. I don't want to be let down if it is about something else."

Helen patted her back. "Then we'll not speak of it again.

Let's finish dressing and pray the time goes quickly."

Claudia hugged both girls and went back to do so. And though she tried she could not help but hope Christina's words were true.

❧

Cameron could not believe it when George informed him that morning that Aurora was waiting for him in the salon. A dread fell over his heart, and he knew whatever she wanted could not be good.

For the last two weeks, ever since their meeting in front of his home, he had searched endlessly for a man who would make an offer for Aurora's hand. He'd even secretly added a substantial dowry to the proposal if only they could see the deed done.

Yet one by one those he could persuade to go through with the plan came back and told him Aurora had denied them.

Finally he went to her cousin's home, where she was living for the season, and met with her. He then asked her why she found none of these suitable, and her answers were all vague, petty reasons. What confounded him was she didn't even seem upset that her time was running out. She just reminded him several times about his promise to marry her.

He had truly begun to fear the outcome of his dealings with Aurora. He lamented to himself over and over about how foolish he'd been to promise something so important.

Especially when the only woman he wanted to be with was Claudia.

As he stood at the door of the salon, he groaned inwardly with regret as he thought of how he'd had to prolong his friendship with Claudia without ever letting her know his true feelings. It was ridiculous really, and yet she seemed to bear it better than any other woman would. Most women, seeking a match, would probably have given up on him and moved on to someone more ready to admit his intentions.

But he sensed a special connection existed between Claudia and him. One that was strong enough, apparently, that she was unwilling to give up on him.

So he'd spent his days with her, trying to act only as a friend, but knowing his actions meant something else.

And then there was George. Cameron glanced about to see if he was still around and was relieved he had gone. George had grown so close to Claudia, and because of Cameron's hesitation the older man was beginning to question his intentions toward his granddaughter.

He could only imagine what his butler was thinking about Aurora's visit this afternoon.

North and every one of his acquaintances had questioned him about Claudia, and even his mother had demanded he not string this out any longer since the ton was starting to speculate on the matter.

It was just that honor and keeping one's word had always been important to him. He'd hoped and prayed for a way out of the promise without having to break his word.

Yet apparently it wasn't to be.

So now there was only one thing to be done.

Taking a deep breath he opened the door and was startled to see Aurora standing there in front of him with tears streaming down her face. Before he could react she ran and threw herself into his arms, crying hysterically.

"Aurora! Will you please get hold of yourself?" he said loudly, pulling her away from him. "Why are you here?"

"Father is here in town," she sobbed, dabbing at her eyes with a lace handkerchief. "He's here to tell Lord Carmichael I will marry him."

Cameron shut the door so her crying would not bring the whole staff down upon them then walked into the room. "I told you you should not have been so particular with the gentlemen who offered for you. You knew time was running out," he chided her, his voice harsh.

She stopped him from sitting down, taking hold of his hand and turning him to look at her. "We still have time," she assured him, her eyes suddenly clear. "All we have to do is go and tell him."

"Tell him what?" he asked faintly, letting go of her hand and taking a few steps away from her.

"That we're betrothed."

She stated those words as if it were the most perfect solution in the world.

"Aurora, I have placated you through this whole situation, but enough is—"

"Let me remind you, my lord, of your promise," she interrupted.

"I know I made that promise, Aurora, but it was only to calm you down. I had every confidence you'd find a husband. And in fact there were several good candidates."

"But none of them would do!" she wailed, stepping closer to him.

Cameron backed up but found his legs had hit against a small table. "Why would you dismiss them but agree to marry me—a man who feels only affection for you, like a sister? I don't love you, Aurora," he told her forcibly and bluntly. "I don't want to marry you—you know this."

Her eyes lowered, but not before he saw the hurt his words had caused. He hated to be so ill-mannered, but he was desperate for her to see the truth.

"We have friendship, Cameron," she said softly, caressing the top of his hand. "In time it will grow into more."

Cameron stared down at her in dismay. "Or we would grow apart, Aurora. Why would you want to marry a man who does not *want* to marry you?"

She lifted her head back up, and he saw that the tears were back. "But you want to marry Lady Claudia, do you not?

Everyone says so." She sniffed and dabbed at her eyes again.

"Actually it is none of your business *who* I want to marry, Aurora," he said wearily, rubbing his finger across his brow. He hated to bring this whole issue about the promise to such an abrupt end since he knew she would be hurt, but he had let this interfere with his life long enough. "Let me be honest with you, Aurora. I cannot marry you. I hate to put it so bluntly, but there it is."

"But what about Lord Carmichael?" she cried, staring at him with a shocked expression.

"I know your father is a hard man, Aurora, but if you protest enough I seriously doubt he shall hold you to such a promise," he told her, fully believing this was true. He'd thought many nights about Lord Wyndham, and though he was quite a humorless man and strict with his only daughter on some things, she was still allowed to do and go anywhere she pleased.

"No, no, he means it, Cameron!" she wailed, grabbing hold of his arm. "Surely you are not so dishonorable that you would go back on your word. You must marry me."

Cameron hated to see women cry, but he did not have the time to console her. Gently he took her hand and pulled it away from his arm. "I'm sorry, Aurora. But you had every chance to save yourself from the fate of Lord Carmichael. I did all a friend could." New tears welled up in her eyes, and she opened her mouth to say something, but he beat her to it. "Now, if you'll excuse me, I have an appointment this evening. George will show you out." He bowed his head then turned to let himself out of the door.

"But, Cameron," she whimpered after him. "I thought we were friends."

Cameron kept walking. The farther he distanced himself from Aurora, the freer he felt. In fact he felt as though he was finally in control of his life again.

He'd strung out his courtship with Claudia because he felt honor bound to resolve this situation with Aurora.

But no more. Tonight he would go to the ball and declare his feelings for her.

His only regret was that he had not done it sooner.

❧

At a few minutes before eight o'clock Cameron stepped onto the Northingshires' terrace. He wanted to avoid the rest of the guests, so he had chosen not to come into the ballroom, instead walking through the garden.

As the cool night breeze blew softly through his hair and brought with it the delicate scent of roses, he leaned against the terrace railing and thought about the object in his vest pocket.

His grandmother's betrothal ring.

Cameron reached up and took the sapphire and diamond ring from his pocket, while imagining Claudia's expression when he would present it to her. Would she be surprised, or would she guess why he wanted to see her tonight?

He heard the sound of muted laughter coming from inside and tucked the ring back into his vest. Carefully he stepped beside the glass-paned, terrace doors and peeked through them. The ball was in full swing with the ladies and gentlemen of the ton dressed in their finest and milling about the room.

He couldn't spot Claudia, though, without bringing attention to himself.

With a sigh he backed up from the window but started when he felt a hand on his back, stopping his progress. He whirled around, ready to confront whoever had sneaked up behind, but stopped short when he saw who it was.

Aurora.

"What are you doing here?" he demanded harshly. He scanned the area to see if anyone was with her or had followed her but found no one.

"I came alone, Cameron," she said. "I followed you here."

He brought his gaze back to her and shook his head. "Why would you do that, Aurora? You know we shouldn't be here alone."

Reaching for his hands, she hugged them to her and stepped closer. He tried to tug free gently, but she held fast. "I came to plead with you to reconsider our agreement. You know you must honor it. 'A man's word is everything,' you once told me," she begged, her eyes wild with desperation.

Cameron felt helpless in knowing how to handle Aurora. Nor could he help but feel responsible for her distracted state. "Aurora, I am deeply sorry you thought I would marry you, but I tried to tell you my feelings all along."

"But I cannot marry Lord Carmichael. Please don't send me to that fate. You cannot be that cruel!" she cried louder.

Panicked, Cameron looked back at the doors and was relieved to find no one seemed to have heard her. Acting more forcibly, he shook his hands away from her and stepped over to the railing. "Aurora, there is nothing you can do or say that will change this. I will not marry you," he stated firmly. "I'm sorry for hurting you, but, promise or no, I will not sacrifice the happiness of both of us on an ill-spoken word."

He expected her to start crying again, but Aurora only stared at him. He wondered if she were trying to decide what tactic to use next. Regardless, he took the momentary pause to glance through the panes of the terrace doors to see if Claudia was near but did not see her.

He looked back at Aurora and saw anger blazing in her eyes. "You are waiting for someone!" she shrieked.

"Aurora, please keep your voice down!" he tried to shush her. But since her head was now directed toward the doors he knew she wasn't listening.

She then turned to glare at him through narrow eyes. "It's Claudia, isn't it? She is the reason you refuse to keep your word. She is—"

"Aurora, please—," he tried again, but to no avail.

"—the woman you want to marry. And please do not say it isn't any of my business, because it is. It is my business," she cried, pointing her finger to her chest as she walked closer to him.

There was a sort of hysterical anger in her expression, and though Cameron tried to back away from her he found himself pinned in the corner of the wall and terrace railing. He had no idea how to handle Aurora—what to say to make her leave. "Aurora, calm down. You are only going to make yourself ill by getting so upset." He tried to soothe her with the only words he could think of.

Apparently those weren't the right ones to say. "Calm down? I had thought you would marry me, and now that you will not, my life is in shambles. How can I calm down?"

Her pitch was getting higher and louder as she now stood within a few inches of him. He had no choice but to reach out and take her by the arms so he could move her back, but she had another plan altogether.

Before he had a good hold of her, she launched herself forward, clasped both arms around his neck, and kissed him on the mouth in a hard, lip-numbing kiss.

The sudden momentum of her embrace knocked him backward over the railing, and he had to wrap both arms around her to pull them both upright again.

At that moment the door of the terrace opened, and he heard a gasp and his name called out in alarm. "Lord Kinclary!"

He finally succeeded in turning his head away from her, but her arms were another matter. Anxiously he glanced over to see both Claudia and Helen standing there staring at him with shock and disbelief.

He grabbed her arms and tried to pry them off his neck. "Aurora!" he exclaimed, glancing at Claudia again, only to find they were no longer alone. "We are being watched."

Several men and women of the ton were stepping out to see

what the commotion was and gasping and gaping when they saw them.

As rapidly as she'd wrapped her arms around him, she let go and jumped away to face the growing crowd. "Oh, dear," she murmured, covering her mouth in surprise.

"This is not what it looks like." He stared straight at Claudia, only to realize how lame his words sounded to everyone around. Snickers rose from the crowd, but he was gazing only at Claudia.

Watching her beautiful eyes fill with hurt and confusion.

Helen was the first to jump into action as she whirled to face her guests. "Ladies and gentlemen, shall we all go back into the ballroom?" she requested firmly and managed to corral them back inside.

Claudia hadn't moved.

"Claudia, please let me explain what happened," he said as he hurried to her. He tried to take her hand, but she jerked it out of his reach.

"No!" she exclaimed in a tortured voice, her eyes swimming with tears. "I saw you kissing her," she whispered, blinking the tears back.

Cameron's own eyes were stinging as the full impact of what had happened began to register with him. "Claudia, Aurora kissed me and—"

Helen interrupted him as she stepped back onto the terrace. "Claudia, I think it best you come inside," she said gently to her friend while she glared at Cameron.

Claudia blinked again and looked at Helen. "I. . .yes," she stammered and let Helen guide her to the door.

"But if I could—," Cameron began again.

"You have to realize the consequences of what just happened here, my lord. Nothing you can say or do will change this," Helen said quietly and then escorted Claudia inside.

fourteen

As soon as they were gone Cameron turned to Aurora, who had stood for the last few minutes uncharacteristically quiet. "What have you done to us?" he asked, as the realization of their situation raced through his mind.

Aurora blinked a few times and looked at him. "Cameron, how was I to know Lady Claudia would be coming out here? You cannot blame me for what has happened." She took a visible breath. "But now that it has, we must consider that it is our destiny, mustn't we? After all, you did make a promise—"

"Enough about that promise!" He waved his hands angrily in the air.

Aurora folded her arms and thrust her chin forward stubbornly. "Yes, I suppose it is a moot point now. As it stands, our reputations have been compromised, though we are *both* blameless. Our engagement must be announced."

As much as Cameron wanted to deny her words, he could not. Aurora was right. They had been compromised.

The incident would be in the gossip column in tomorrow's news. His parents and her father would expect nothing less.

He thought of Claudia's stricken, hurt expression, and he knew he had to explain it all to her. It would bring little comfort to her, though, he imagined. Whether she suspected him of being unfaithful or knew the truth of Aurora's emotional display that had ruined them both, the end result was the same.

He must marry Aurora.

How could one moment change their futures, their hopes and dreams?

And separate him from Claudia forever?

"We must go in there and announce it tonight," Aurora said beside him, her voice urgent as she pointed toward the glass doors that led back into the ballroom. "You know we must."

Cameron looked up and saw several people standing by the door, watching them, and suddenly felt a deep sadness rise within his heart. All his life Cameron had lived honorably and above reproach. He'd always been careful about the friends he chose and the places he went because he knew that any sort of gossip or scandal would reflect on his family's name.

Now he was bound to marry a woman he did not love and was being gawked at like a circus animal by his peers.

He could only be thankful that neither his parents nor Aurora's father was in attendance, for they surely would be mortified by the whole affair.

"We have to make it seem as though we'd planned to announce the engagement all along and not as a result of what happened here earlier," Cameron finally spoke, thinking aloud.

"I agree," Aurora answered.

He took in a deep breath and held out his arm to Aurora. "Let's see this deed done then."

He felt like a condemned man walking the path to his own execution. He plastered on a smile he could never feel as they pushed their way through the curious members of the ton and wondered why God had allowed this to happen.

Was this His will? Did God have a purpose for his marrying Aurora? If so, Cameron prayed it would be revealed to him, for he needed to understand.

"I need to speak with the Northingshires to prepare them for the announcement," he said as they walked the perimeter of the room. He finally spotted them, but his heart sank when he saw Claudia standing beside them.

"There they are," Aurora said, pointing in their direction.

"Perhaps you'd better stand here and let me handle this

alone," Cameron said. He owed it to Claudia to give her an explanation before he made the announcement.

"Absolutely not!" Aurora cried softly, gripping his arm tighter. "You cannot leave me to bear their scrutiny alone. See how their judging eyes condemn me already?"

"Then you should have thought about this before you threw yourself at me," he hissed and discreetly pulled her arms away from him. "Stay here against the wall, and I'll be back in a moment."

"But—," he heard Aurora say. But he ignored her pleading tone as he made his way to where his friends stood.

North noticed him first. He felt a pang of remorse when he saw the duke tense and frown with marked censure. "North, I must speak with you—all of you," he told them quickly, looking them each in the eye until he finally came to Claudia. "I especially need to explain what you saw out there on the terrace."

Claudia narrowed her eyes at him. The hurt he'd seen earlier in her expression had now been replaced by anger. "Explain what? That I'm not the only girl you go about kissing?"

"Claude, I wasn't kissing her. I—"

"Don't call me Claude, you rogue!" she hissed.

"Kinclary, before you draw more attention to yourself, perhaps we'd better go somewhere private so you can tell me what you mean to do now," North insisted in a soft but serious tone.

Nodding, he followed all three of them into a small room off the ballroom. Once they were closed inside he tried to get Claudia to look at him, but she stubbornly looked away. Finally Cameron pulled his gaze away from Claudia and looked at North. "I must announce that Aurora and I are to be wed," he said bluntly. He heard Claudia gasp but forced himself to continue. "We must make it seem as though we'd planned to announce it all along. It's the only way to keep scandal at bay."

North nodded. "I agree. There were too many witnesses, and the news has spread quickly amongst our guests."

"Wait a moment." Claudia stepped closer. "You are going to marry Aurora because you were caught embracing her?"

Cameron sighed, wishing he did not have to put her through this pain. "Is it not the way of things in American society also? If I do not marry her, in time I could recover from it simply because I am a man and heir to an exalted title—but not before my family and sisters experienced the censure and judgment of the ton. Aurora, however, would suffer from the shame all her life and have little chance for marriage." Cameron stared with pleading eyes at Claudia. "You know this must be done."

The anger drained from Claudia's face, leaving her pale. "If only someone had caught our kiss—," she murmured, as if she couldn't help speaking it.

"Yes," he interrupted in a gruff voice. He would not let her finish the sentence for he couldn't bear to think about it.

All of a sudden the door opened, and Aurora stepped inside. "Did you tell them our happy news?" she asked cheerfully, nudging her way between Claudia and him. Aurora was quick to grab hold of his arm and hug it to her in a familiar fashion. A gesture that did not go unnoticed by the Northingshires or Claudia.

"Aurora, please. You need not playact in front of my friends."

He should have known Aurora would do as she pleased. With a pout she reached with her other hand to pat his arm. "Then they must realize we have known each other since childhood. No one can be surprised that our marriage is a natural progression of our long friendship."

Shaking his head with frustration, Cameron got back to the point of his and North's earlier conversation. "Shall we make the announcement now? The sooner the better, I think."

They exited the room, and North got to it straightaway, quieting the orchestra and making the announcement. Aurora played her part to the hilt as the adoring fiancée clinging to his arm and gazing up into his eyes. Cameron remembered smiling and hoping it would convince the masses they had been planning this announcement all along.

And it worked. A few cast suspicious glances in their direction, but mostly everyone forgave their earlier imprudent display and accepted that two good English families were about to be united.

Claudia had her own part to play in the affair. She had to stand and smile, pretending she was happy with the announcement. For her to show anything else would cause the ton to speculate that he threw Claudia over for Aurora. They'd been seen together so much in public that there would still be speculation, but if she maintained they were only friends the matter would soon be forgotten.

He hated that she had to bear any sort of censure. She was innocent in all of this, and he blamed himself for not doing something to stop it.

If only he'd dealt with Aurora earlier. If only he'd never made that thoughtless promise to begin with.

If only—

"Dear God, please be with Claudia," he whispered aloud as he watched her walk about the room with Helen at her side.

"What did you say?" Aurora asked, bringing his attention back to her.

He shook his head and let out a sigh. "I believe we should go and speak to your father," he said instead of answering her question and began to walk toward the door.

They were in the process of collecting their coat, shawl, and hats when he turned once more to glance about the room.

Claudia must have sensed she was being watched, for her gaze connected with his across the brightly lit ballroom. But she only held it for a second before turning and walking in the opposite direction from him.

"Must we go, Cam? The prince regent will be insulted we left before he has even arrived," Aurora complained with another one of her usual pouts.

"I suspect he will recover quickly," Cameron said wearily, escorting her into the hallway and then out of the house.

Time seemed to be running faster than normal, for they arrived at her residence before he knew it. Lord Wyndham, a tall austere gentleman who rarely smiled, soon joined them in the room where they'd been waiting. He was dressed in his usual black suit of clothes, which made him seem even more remote and cold. Cameron remembered seeing him several times at Rosehaven Castle but could not recall ever holding a significant conversation with him.

He had no idea how the older man would react to the news.

"This is rather a late hour for a visit, Kinclary," he stated after they'd bowed and exchanged polite greetings. Cameron saw the man's gaze move to his daughter standing beside him. Suspicion was evident in his expression. "Aurora, am I to assume you arrived here with Kinclary? Alone?"

Cameron glanced at Aurora and saw she was nervously wringing her hands. "Y—yes. We. . .uh. . .he took me home from the Northingshire ball, Papa," she stammered.

"I shall get right to the point of this visit, my lord. Aurora and I were. . .conversing on the terrace and were caught in a compromising position that was witnessed by several guests," he explained, oversimplifying the scene.

Wyndham's whole demeanor changed into something dark and foreboding. "And what sort of *compromising position* was it?" he asked through gritted teeth.

"Just a simple embrace, Papa. That was all," Aurora answered in an innocent tone.

But Cameron knew the particulars of what happened would get around to him sooner or later, and he would rather not have his future father-in-law think he was a deceiver. "A kiss was involved as well," he added.

From the corner of his eye he saw Aurora glare up at him.

"I see," Lord Wyndham said in a low voice. By the way he narrowed his gaze at them both, Cameron had an inkling he saw much more than was actually the truth. "And if you were not caught? Would you mean to misuse my daughter, my lord, and not do right by her?"

The moment seemed so otherworldly that Cameron felt as though he were watching the whole scene as an audience watched a play. Had he ever imagined he would be put in such a position? He had not.

"Of course not, my lord. I can state truthfully that I have never touched your daughter in an untoward fashion and have always treated her with respect," Cameron said.

"Until tonight," Wyndham reminded him with a flat tone.

Cameron glanced again at Aurora, but she avoided his eyes. *What did I expect,* he wondered, *that she'd speak up and tell the truth of the whole matter?* "Yes, until tonight," he answered.

The muscle in Lord Wyndham's jaw jerked about as if he were trying to hold on to his anger. "And now what is to be done?" Wyndham drew his words out slowly, much like a judge sentencing a man to his doom.

"I've come to make an offer. . .to marry your daughter," Cameron said, almost choking on those last words.

"And I would expect no less." Wyndham said no more for a moment but continued to study them both.

Cameron fought the urge to reach up and loosen his cravat so that he could breath easier.

"Come back this week, and we will settle the arrangements. I hope you will not expect a large dowry from Aurora, for I am only able to give her twenty pounds a year."

Cameron nodded to the older man. "That will be fine, my lord."

"Good night," he said with finality as he turned stiffly and walked toward the door. "Aurora?" he called without turning.

Aurora sent Cameron an apologetic look, then ran after him, leaving Cameron alone in the room.

He stood there for a few minutes, trying to reason how all of this could have happened and how he could have prevented it.

But it was a waste of time and energy. The facts were the facts. He would be marrying a woman who did not share his beliefs in God nor his passion for ministry and helping the poor.

Why had God allowed this? Cameron wondered for the umpteenth time that night. Was this what He wanted for him? If only Cameron knew the reason, he could live with himself a little better.

As it was, he blamed himself for making the promise that started this whole affair. If he had not, it would be he and Claudia who would be celebrating their engagement on this night.

Now he must squelch the love he felt for her and remind himself every day that she could only be his friend.

And even that may not be possible.

fifteen

"Claudia, are you sure you want to go to the shelter today?" Helen sat in the backseat of their carriage with Claudia as North drove them to the waterfront. "I can teach your class if this is what troubles you."

Claudia had almost sent a note to Helen asking her that very thing, but something inside would not let her do it. She did not volunteer her time at the shelter just to spend time with Cameron. This was the work God had led her to, and she would not shirk her responsibilities because of a broken heart.

And, too, there was her grandfather Canterbury. She didn't want him to think all her efforts to get to know him were only a ploy to be near his employer.

No. Going to the shelter was the only way to pick up the pieces of her life and move on. It would be hard to be around Cameron knowing he belonged to someone else now, but she was strong.

God had a purpose in all of this, of that she was sure. She would have to depend on Him to show her His will and the next step she should take in life.

"I have to do this, Helen. Those children depend on me, and I think I need them also. Life goes on, and I will be more productive if I get out there and work," she told her friend kindly.

Helen sighed and searched Claudia's face. "I'm just worried about your seeing Cameron. You both love each other so—"

"Helen! Please don't keep reminding me," she pleaded, gently holding on to her arm.

"Oh, I'm so sorry," she cried, covering Claudia's hand. "I'm terrible at knowing the right thing to say."

Claudia smiled at her. "You both being here with me and supporting me is enough."

But her brave words faded away the moment she stepped into the shelter and saw Cameron holding one of the children.

An awkward moment passed between them, but one that was smoothed over by William, the child in Cameron's arms. The little boy held out his finger, which was wrapped with a bulky bandage, and said, "Lord Kinclary made my finger better, miss."

Everyone laughed, and Claudia walked up to take the child from him. Cameron smiled down at her, and she was able to return it with little effort.

Turning her attention to the boy's finger, she said, "That is quite a large bandage, William. Is it holding your finger together?"

Cameron scratched his head and smiled sheepishly. "It's actually a small scratch, but it's the best I could do."

Claudia shook her head at him and started to take the child to the classroom when Cameron stopped her with his words.

"I didn't think you'd come back."

She closed her eyes briefly, praying for strength. Turning back to him, she countered, "I'll leave. . .if you prefer it."

His eyes widened. "No! I mean, of course I want you to stay. You have a heart for these people and this work as much as I do. My. . .*situation*. . .doesn't change this." He stumbled over his last sentence.

She breathed a sigh of relief. "Then I'll be happy to continue on." William began to wiggle about in her arms, so she set him down and watched him run toward the class.

"Excellent," he replied, bringing Claudia's attention back to him. "I want you to know the truth about the embrace you saw last night," he said next.

Claudia felt a panic rise within her. Perhaps it was wrong of her, but she could not discuss Aurora with him. "No, please, Cameron. It doesn't matter," she told him firmly as she turned away.

"She threw herself into my arms in a fit of emotion because I refused to marry her," he said quickly.

Claudia stopped and turned back to him. "What?"

Cameron took a breath then told her about Aurora's dilemma of needing to find a husband and the promise he'd made to marry her if she could not find someone within the month. "She came to my home last night before the ball. She told me I must honor my promise to marry her since her father had threatened to marry her to Lord Carmichael."

Claudia's eyes widened as a picture of the old, toothless nobleman filled her mind. "He would have her marry such an old man?"

Cameron shook his head. "This is what she told me; yet when I spoke to her father last night, he never mentioned Lord Carmichael. Perhaps it was an empty threat to make Aurora choose a husband."

"And she chose you?" she asked although she knew the answer in her heart. It was clear last night how Aurora felt about him.

"She will not admit it, but I think she wanted me to marry her all along." Cameron ran his hand through his hair and sighed wearily. "I cannot help but share some responsibility for her feelings. I spent time with her and took her to balls when I came home on holidays, believing we were only friends. She apparently felt more."

Claudia, as much as she loathed admitting it, could see how Aurora could love him although her feelings were not reciprocated. Cameron was unlike any man she had ever known. "And you told her you would honor your promise to her?" she asked, getting back to his story.

"No!" Cameron exclaimed, lifting his hands out to his sides.

"I told her I had made that promise hastily and without thought. Though she may have thought me dishonorable, I was not going to let one promise, made in haste, ruin my life. In truth I knew Aurora could probably find a way out of the situation with her father." He stopped and looked at her with sadness. "There was also another reason why I broke my promise to her. But it will do us both no good to speak of it."

Claudia looked away from him and willed herself not to cry. She had done enough of that the night before. "No, it won't," she said faintly. Curiosity gave her enough fortitude to bring her gaze back to him. "And last night? On the terrace?"

"I was waiting for you when she suddenly walked out onto the terrace. She was crying and begging me to uphold my promise to her. I was trying to tell her I would not change my mind when she suddenly launched herself into my arms." His face became grim. "Then you and your friends walked out at that moment. Even then it might have been all right, but when Helen called out my name—"

"It brought out half our guests to witness your embrace," Claudia finished for him.

"It was not an embrace on my part. I had to put my arms around her to stop her from knocking us both down to the stone floor when she kissed me." He put his hands in his pockets and looked at the ground then finally back to Claudia. "In doing so I sealed my fate forever."

"Oh, Cameron," she cried softly. "Why has this happened? I was so sure God had a different plan for me—for us."

"So did I," he agreed, his voice rough with emotion.

They stared at one another for a long moment, and Claudia knew what she must say next. But it was so difficult to do. "What's done is done. We must believe God has everything in control, and it is according to His will this has happened. I shall pray for both you and Aurora."

A pained look crossed Cameron's face, but it was fleeting.

He gave her a small smile that seemed as though it took great effort and nodded his head. "It is exactly as I have reasoned also. I will pray for you as well."

Claudia swallowed, trying to push down the knot that was rising in her throat, and nodded. "I had better attend to my class," she said and made her way to the classroom before he could respond.

Though Claudia thought she'd have a hard time concentrating on her pupils that morning, it turned out to be quite the opposite. As she helped them with their work, she was able to focus on something worthwhile, instead of reliving what had taken place the night before.

God did have a purpose for her meeting Cameron, and though it wasn't for the ultimate reason she'd longed for, she had found her dear grandfather Canterbury and discovered a way to help those less fortunate than her.

She had to keep believing He would ease the pain of seeing Cameron every day, while knowing he could never be with her.

Both she and Mrs. Owen were lining up the children to eat their noonday meal when her grandfather stepped into the doorway and asked to see her in his office.

As she followed him the short distance she tried to gauge his demeanor. Had he heard the news of Cameron and Aurora? If so, how upset was he? His face gave her no answers, however, for it remained set in the calm expression he always wore. Claudia liked to call it his butler's face, for each one she'd come across wore the same look.

Once inside, her grandfather showed her to a seat and sat in his chair stationed behind his desk. She didn't realize she was still staring at him so hard until he demanded, "Why do you stare at me so intently, Claudia? Have I something on my face?"

Claudia blinked. "I do apologize, Grandpapa, but I was just trying to see how you were taking the news about Cameron."

George shook his head in confusion. "Are you speaking of his making me the president of this shelter and charity?"

"What?" Claudia gasped. "When did he do this?"

"Last night he came by and—" He stopped and looked at her. "You don't know, do you? What news were you speaking of then?"

Claudia was not pleased with the fact she would have to tell him about Cameron's impromptu engagement. How could he not know if he lived in the same house as his employer? Stalling, Claudia said, "Why don't you tell me your news first?"

Her grandfather stared at her for a moment. Finally he explained, "Last night his lordship informed me the duties of the shelter were growing too large for us not to have a manager present all day. So, as of this morning, I am no longer employed as his lordship's butler but am now the chairman of the London Riverhouse Shelter," he announced. "He told me I could lease an apartment his family owns in Hanover Square, off Bruton Street. I've been moving all morning and have not had a chance to speak to anyone."

Claudia felt so proud of her grandfather and so deeply thankful to Cameron for giving him this chance. She had a suspicion he might have done it partly for her, but she was grateful just the same. "That's wonderful, Grandpapa. I'll have to come and help you get settled into your new residence."

The older man nodded but laid his papers to the side and gazed at her. "So what is your news?"

She had to take a moment to get her emotions under control. What she wanted to do was throw herself into his warm embrace and cry her eyes out, but she wouldn't do that. She'd cried for several hours through the night, and when morning had finally come she became determined to keep her emotions under control for the rest of the day.

"Lord Kinclary has become engaged to Lady Aurora," she told him.

"He what?" her grandfather roared, standing, his expression fierce and thunderous. "I knew the woman was up to no good when she called on his lordship yesterday. And Kinclary—what right has he to play false with your feelings while pledging himself to another?"

Claudia held out her hand in supplication. "Please, Grandpapa. Sit down. Let me tell you all that has transpired."

She quickly repeated what Cameron had told her. When she was done, she noticed her grandfather had grown quiet and thoughtful.

"Lady Aurora has been manipulating his lordship ever since they were children. I never understood why he couldn't see through her whining and false tears," her grandfather recalled.

Claudia sighed and knew it would do no good to speak ill of Aurora. "That is neither here nor there, Grandpapa. Should she have thrown herself into Cameron's arms as she did? Probably not. But I know she was distraught over his refusal to honor the promise to marry her. Perhaps she was not herself last night."

"You are being very kind to the woman who is to marry the man you love," he said gently.

Claudia looked away for a moment. "I cannot lie and say that part of me doesn't feel resentful toward her, but I am trying to live as the Bible teaches. I read this morning in Ephesians chapter four, verse thirty-two, 'And be ye kind one to another, tenderhearted, forgiving one another, even as God for Christ's sake hath forgiven you.' I memorized it so I might remind myself of it all during day."

Her grandfather smiled at her. "You know, Claudia—after your mother eloped with your father I had stopped praying to God, and rarely did I attend church." He drew in a deep breath as he gazed about his room. "But when I began helping his lordship with the shelter, I felt compelled to start attending again because Lord Kinclary seemed to have such a desire to do God's will in his life. And then you came into my life, and I began praying to God, thanking Him for bringing you into my life—even though I was a bit stubborn about the matter at first," he added with a self-deprecating grin.

"I can truly endure this pain in my heart then, knowing it has brought us together and both closer to God," she said sincerely and gratefully, stretching her hand across his desk.

Her grandfather covered it with his own hand, and Claudia felt immediately comforted by his touch. "Indeed, my dear. I just wish you did not have to endure such sadness and heartbreak. Can't I do something?"

Claudia shook her head and stood. "There is nothing to be done. But I do want you to know how proud I am about your new position."

"Thank you, my dear," he said as he stood with her. "You'll come to me if you need anything, won't you?"

"Of course. But I will still be seeing you everyday."

Her grandfather's brows rose in surprise. "You will continue your work here? Do you think it wise?"

Claudia couldn't be sure about anything at this point. With a sigh she shook her head and answered, "I don't know, Grandpapa. But I do not want to stop my work with these children. I've come to care so much for them."

Her grandfather nodded, but he still seemed troubled. He came around the desk and walked her to the door. "As I said, I am here for you, Claudia. You can always depend on that."

She smiled and put her arms around him. He only hesitated a moment before returning her hug, and that widened Claudia's smile. Though he still was not used to affection, he was learning quickly.

"Thank you, Grandpapa," she whispered against his coat.

✿

Cameron tried to pretend he wasn't just standing around in the hallway waiting for Claudia and George to finish their meeting. Yet that was precisely what he was about, ever since he had seen them enter the office and close the door behind them.

He knew he should have been the one to tell George about the engagement, but he could not seem to form the words this morning when he'd awakened his butler from his bed. He'd instead offered him the job of running the shelter full-time. He'd been thinking about promoting him all along, of course; but because of the devastation he felt over the engagement, he wanted to feel good about *something*.

Just then the door to George's office opened. Cameron headed in that direction and hoped it appeared as though he were passing by on the way to somewhere else.

He had reached the door when Claudia stepped out.

"Oh! Cameron!" she exclaimed. She glanced back at her grandfather's office and then at him. "What are you doing?"

That is the question, isn't it? He couldn't very well say he'd been skulking through the hallway hoping to find out how George took the news. "I was just—," he began then stopped when he couldn't think of anything to say. "What are you doing?" he countered, folding his arms.

"Oh, well. . ." She hesitated. "I was just talking to Grandpapa about his new job. Thank you for that. You could not have bestowed such a position on a man more appreciative."

He waited a moment for Claudia to elaborate, but she said nothing else. "He is the best man for the job since he worked as hard as I on building this shelter. It is I who feels fortunate and appreciative." He cleared his throat, trying to figure a way to form his next question. "And that is all you talked about?"

Claudia looked at him. "If you are asking if I told him about your engagement, the answer is yes. What I don't understand is why you didn't tell him yourself."

Cameron sighed and rubbed his finger along his chin. "I don't know, Claudia. When I talked with him I'd just returned from speaking with Aurora's father, and frankly I was sick and tired of speaking of the whole sordid affair. Telling George of his promotion was a pleasant alternative to the other business, I suppose."

Claudia looked away. "I can understand that." She glanced back at him. "Well, I'd better go and check on my class. They will be finishing their lunch, and I've yet to have my own."

"Wait," he called out softly, and she turned back to him. "How did your grandfather take the news of. . .the engagement?" Cameron could not bring himself to say "my engagement."

She looked away again. "Think how you would feel if your sister came to you with the same situation." She disappeared then into the classroom.

He stood there in the middle of the hallway, thinking. He had, in fact, gone through a similar situation with his sister when her fiancé broke their engagement only weeks before the wedding. It had been frustrating to see that her heart was breaking and not be able to do anything about it.

George had to be feeling the same way.

So it was with some trepidation he knocked on George's door and stepped into his office.

All it took was one look at his face to see that George knew the whole story. "May I have a moment to speak with you, George?" Cameron asked, half expecting the older man to throw him out on his ear.

George didn't answer right away but took a few deep breaths. Cameron swallowed hard and almost walked back out of the room.

"Of course, my lord," he finally answered, motioning toward the chair across from his desk.

After Cameron was seated, he got right to the subject. "You know, do you not? About my engagement?"

George nodded gravely. "Indeed, my lord."

Cameron sighed and ran his hand through his hair. "I know you must be sorely vexed with me at this moment, George, but it cannot be worse than I feel about myself." He looked away and prayed for guidance. "It is all my fault. I made a promise in haste to keep Aurora from worrying me with her situation, and then when I told her I would not marry her, she came to the ball to find me. I should have escorted her into the ballroom straight away. She might have thought twice about launching herself at me then."

"While it is true you should not have made the promise in the first place, it is hardly your fault that you were caught in such a position. How could you have known what she would do?"

"Regardless, we were caught, and our reputations compromised," he said deliberately, more to remind himself. He turned his head to stare out of the window to his right. "I never believed when she came to me with her dilemma that it would come to this."

"Surely you can see now that she never meant for this to go any other way, my lord. You have been friends for years, and while you always regarded her as a sister, her feelings were quite the opposite. This fact was obvious to me when she came to your home last night."

Cameron jerked his gaze back to George. "Why could I not have seen this? How could I be blind to the fact that she felt this affection for me?"

The older man strummed his fingers on his desk. "You probably saw what you *wanted* to see, my lord. You felt no such attachment to her, so you ignored the signs that were there."

Cameron ran his hand through his hair again as he absorbed George's words. "I feel like such a fool," he said wearily.

George looked at him with concern. "We all make mistakes, my lord. You must forgive yourself."

"But this has affected not only my life, George, but Claudia's and yours, not to mention our families and friends. My only consolation is that I will have a few months to get used to the idea of having to marry Aurora."

"I'm afraid you don't even have that to comfort you, my lord." George picked up the *Times* he had laid on his desk and handed it to him.

Cameron raised his brow then looked down at the column George had indicated. His heart felt as though it had dropped down to his toes when he saw his name in print next to Aurora's. "It's a wedding announcement," he murmured.

"Yes, your own," George said.

Cameron glanced at him, then at the paper. It announced their wedding would take place in three weeks.

For the announcement to be printed today, Aurora had to have submitted it yesterday morning, right after he'd spoken to her and told her he couldn't marry her.

Cameron's stomach clenched. Last night before she left the ball she had asked him to set a date. He had put her off saying he would have to think about it.

But she had already set it.

"I'm sorry, my lord," George said quietly. "But I thought it was something you had to see."

Cameron folded the paper and tucked it inside his coat. "I was feeling terribly sorry for myself last night. I knelt at my bedside and asked the Lord over and over why this had happened to me. It was a selfish prayer and one I am not proud of, but God heard me just the same." He leaned forward in his chair, his elbows braced on his knees. "I was reminded of what Christ went through before He was nailed to the cross and then what the disciples endured while they endeavored to spread the good news to all the lands. I felt contrite, of course. But then I also felt blessed. God has given me so much in my life. Why am I to throw a tantrum when things do not go my way?"

"We all grow through adversity," George added.

Cameron nodded, looking down at his hands. "Yes." Taking

a deep breath, he clapped his hands together and rose from his chair. "Well, enough said about this. We still have a shelter to run and people to look after."

George stood with him. "Indeed we do, my lord."

Cameron smiled at the older man, grateful for the friendship they shared. "Thank you for speaking with me." He nodded his head and started toward the door.

He took hold of the door handle but stopped and turned once more to George. "My greatest regret in all this is the hurt I have caused Claudia, George. I would never have started a relationship with her had I known—"

"I never thought you would, my lord. You have no need to explain."

Cameron nodded as the pain of losing Claudia washed over him once more; then he left the room.

sixteen

Two weeks later Claudia entered her bedroom with Helen after a tiring dinner party at Lord Paisley's home. She admitted to Helen that it was becoming a strain to be around Cameron.

"Helen, we have attended every ball, soirée, dinner party, and even a boring poetry reading, and still I cannot stop thinking about him. Not when I see him every day at the shelter."

She walked to the window and plopped down on the cushioned window seat overlooking St. James Square.

"I was hoping you'd meet some other gentleman who could make you forget about your heartbreak. But then I think about my love for North and know it could not be that easy." Helen sat down beside her and started picking the pins out of her hair.

Claudia sat up and motioned for Helen to turn so she could do it for her. "I feel as if I spend all my free time praying God will show me what to do next. I admit I cannot hear His answer. Do I stay at the shelter where I am helping others, or do I try to find another venue? I do not know."

Helen sighed. "What about your grandfather Moreland? Is he still upset with you over losing Cameron to Aurora?"

Claudia brushed through Helen's curls with her fingers. "Not as much. I had contemplated telling him the whole truth of the matter—the shelter, Aurora's throwing herself at Cameron—everything. But it would not change anything."

Helen turned and looked at her with worry. "Claudia, you cannot tell him about the shelter! You know he would stop you from going there."

"I know. Do not be alarmed, Helen. I said I only thought about it."

Helen turned and made a spinning motion with her finger. She then proceeded to take down Claudia's hair. "And the Scotsman? Is your grandfather still talking about him?"

Claudia winced not only from Helen's yanking her hair, but also because of Lord Charles MacBain, the Baron of Glenfalloch. "Unfortunately, yes. Every time we meet, he gives me a glowing description of the baron's vast holdings in Scotland and his exalted political position in the House of Lords."

"What of his looks? Is he old? Young? Does he play the bagpipes and wear a kilt?"

Claudia laughed. "I have no idea, and I haven't asked. It would just encourage Grandfather. My only consolation is that the baron is apparently staying in Scotland for the season and not able to come for a visit."

Helen drew a brush through Claudia's hair. "But what if this highlander is the one for you? The vicar this past Sunday said that God does work in mysterious ways."

Claudia turned back around with her dark hair falling about her shoulders. "They would have to be mysterious, indeed, to make me forget. . ." Her voice trailed off when she realized she was about to mention Cameron again.

Helen gave her a sympathetic smile and patted her hand. "I know."

ช

Cameron had only one week before he would no longer be a single man. One week before all hope for him and Claudia would be gone and he'd be left with a life not of his choosing.

One week before he would no longer come to the shelter on a daily basis.

He'd honestly thought he could do it. He thought he and Claudia could work as friends because they were spreading the love of God to the unfortunate, work that was good and noble. But being with Claudia only made him aware of what he couldn't have.

And Claudia probably thought she was handling things by avoiding him and treating him like a stranger. But they were apparently only kidding themselves.

So he waited by the door, and when she walked in with the Northingshires he stepped up to greet her.

"Hello, Claudia. Do you mind meeting with me a moment in my office?" he said right away, though she wouldn't bring her gaze up to meet his.

"I'm sorry, Cameron, but I have so many things to do—"

"Please. It will take only a moment, and it's important," he insisted.

Something in his voice must have alerted her he was serious, for she looked up at him with wary, questioning eyes. "All right."

He led her quickly into his office and motioned for her to take a seat.

"No, Cameron. Just say what you need to say."

Cameron looked at her rigid posture—the way she had trouble meeting his gaze—and his heart broke all over again.

"You've been avoiding me," he began, not sure why he'd spoken it aloud. It wasn't what he meant to say at all.

She glanced at him then down at the floor. "You know why. I thought you understood why I—"

"I know," he said softly and let out a breath of frustration. "This is why I've made the decision to let George and North handle the running of the shelter."

This time she looked right at him, her eyes filled with dismay. "What? But you can't! This is your dream, your vision, Cameron." She took a step closer. "Don't let her do this! Don't let Aurora keep you from fulfilling God's purpose in your life."

"Aurora is not the reason," he insisted firmly, holding up his hand. "She doesn't like for me to work here, but it isn't why I can't be here anymore."

She shook her head. "Then why? What is so important to make you quit your work?"

He didn't answer for a moment. He looked into her eyes, hoping she would understand how hard it was even being in the same room with her. "You are," he told her bluntly.

Her eyes filled with tears, and she pressed her mouth with her hand. She tried to speak, but the tears seemed to clog her throat.

Cameron had to swallow to clear the lump in his own throat and struggled to stay strong. "It's tearing us apart, Claudia, to be here day after day with each other. You think by avoiding me you can pretend I'm not here. Let us be honest—you are as aware of me as I am you."

She took a deep breath and wiped her cheeks. "Then I will be the one to leave, Cameron," she insisted, her voice broken. "I will not be able to live with myself if I let you give this up for me."

"Claudia, I—"

"No," she said firmly, holding out her hand. "This is your shelter, the vision God gave you. I was only sharing it. I will find another charity to help."

"Absolutely not, Claudia," he returned as firmly. "You and your grandfather can work together and—"

"Grandpapa and I will be fine, Cameron. We've grown very close, and this will change nothing."

"Please, Claudia. Stay."

But he could see her mind was made up. "No, Cameron," she said softly and backed toward the door.

"But—," he began, but she was already walking out of the room.

❧

Claudia had closed Cameron's door and turned when she noticed someone was standing in her path. She couldn't have been more shocked if she'd seen the prince regent himself standing there.

It was Aurora.

"What are you doing here?" Aurora hissed, anger seething

from her expression and voice.

Claudia swallowed, unsure of what to do or say. "I. . .uh. . ."

"Have you been seeing Cameron behind my back? We are not even wed, and he is already playing me for a fool?" she asked, louder this time.

Claudia glanced about the hall and was thankful to find no one about. "Your assumptions are wrong, Aurora. I work here with the children," she told her quickly.

Aurora narrowed her eyes at her. "I don't believe that for one moment. You are here for Cameron. You can't deny that."

Claudia knew Aurora was on her way to causing another scene. "I can and will, Aurora. Now please lower your voice. There are many people about." She took her arm and pulled her further down the hallway, but Aurora shook off her hand after a few steps.

Brushing away her arm as if Claudia's touch offended her, she said, "Say whatever you will. It won't matter anyway once Cameron and I are wed. I shall demand that he give up this—this place. It is not fitting for a man of his position to be doing charity work. It is beneath him."

Claudia could only stare at Aurora after she had spoken those selfish words. She shook her head slowly. "If you truly knew him, you would never demand such a thing. He does this not for his own benefit but because he believes God has purposed him to do it. Do you know where these women would be if not for Cameron? Begging in the streets or possibly dead now. Instead they are learning skills and finding employment in homes and shops to support their children." She paused to take a deep breath and saw that Aurora had stopped scowling and was listening to her. "Preventing him from running this shelter would be to tell him that neither he nor God matters at all. Only you do."

Aurora looked away and folded her arms across her chest. "I don't understand his need to be so religious," she murmured, and Claudia could tell she still did not grasp it.

"It is not religion, Aurora. He loves God and wants to do His will. It is the reason the Duke and Duchess of Northingshire work here also."

Aurora seemed surprised at hearing this. "Oh? I did not realize they were involved also. Cameron has never mentioned you nor them to me."

"We all have to be careful of our reputations. You cannot imagine that I would be here without a friend or chaperone."

Aurora unfolded her arms and rubbed her hand across her brow. "I've imagined many things; yet nothing has turned out as I believed it would," she answered faintly. She must have realized how her words sounded, for she thrust her chin back up and refolded her arms. "I mean I never imagined Cameron had such ideas as this shelter."

Claudia knew that if she were changing anything about Aurora's way of thinking, the woman would be loath to admit it. "Aurora, we have not been friends, and I know you resent my friendship with Cameron, but please be assured of this—he is an upright and honorable man. If he were not, he would have left the ball that night and let you bear the humiliation alone." She stopped for a minute and prayed she would not cry while speaking her next words. "If you are to have any sort of happy. . . marriage, you cannot fight with him on this issue of the shelter. I pray you will read the scriptures or perhaps talk to your vicar and understand for yourself what it means to desire to do the work of the Lord—to follow His will. It will go a long way in helping. . .your marriage be a successful one."

Knowing she could say no more without breaking down, she said, "I must go," and bobbed a curtsy before stepping around her.

Aurora stopped her. "Why are you telling me this? I know you wanted to marry him. All of London knows this." She shook her head. "Yet here you are advising me on how to make him happy. Why would you do this?"

Tears finally filled her eyes as Claudia looked at the woman who was to marry the man she loved. "Because, though he can never be mine, I do want him to be happy and contented in life." She felt a tear splatter on her cheek, but she did nothing to wipe it away. "And you need not worry about me again. I will no longer be working here after today."

She turned, ran down the hall before Aurora could say anymore, and didn't stop until she reached the supply room. Finding a quiet corner she sat down on a wooden crate.

And cried one last time.

≈

As Claudia rode with her friends back to her home that afternoon, she contemplated her options. There seemed to be only one solution—one that would help mend her heart. "Helen, I think I want to go home," she said out of the blue, looking at her friend with resolve.

Helen smiled at her and patted her hand. "That is where we're going, Claudia. I knew you didn't want to go to my house."

Claudia shook her head. "No, I mean I want to go home— to Louisiana."

"Oh!" Helen exclaimed. "If you need to get away, we have a home in Scotland where you are more than welcome to stay and—"

She put her hand over Helen's, stopping her speech. "I want to go home for a while and see my family. It's not forever— only until I know I can face Cameron without breaking down and crying."

Helen nodded, and after discussing the matter further both she and North agreed to go with her and approach her grandfather about it.

It wasn't easy convincing the marquis she would return to fulfill her duties as his heir. In the end, however, he did agree to pay for her voyage.

Lord Moreland was able to find her passage on a ship leaving in three days. Since the captain's wife was on board and agreed to act as her companion, she did not need to find someone to travel with her as a chaperone.

Helen suggested, since North was leaving for a few days on business, that she come and stay with her until she sailed. Claudia agreed, but only if they could stay in and not attend any gatherings.

She did not want to risk seeing Cameron one more time.

seventeen

On the last day before his wedding Cameron found he could not concentrate on his work. Nor did it help matters when George had told him that morning about Claudia leaving for America. After trying to add the same column of numbers four times and getting four different answers, he finally pushed his book of accounts away and walked out to the pier in the back of the shelter.

He leaned against the rough wood of the railing and took a moment to pray. He first thanked God for not only helping him better accept the future that was now laid out before him but for the amazing change in Aurora. He didn't understand what had come over her, but she suddenly stopped arguing with him about the shelter and started acting genuinely interested in what he was doing. She told him also that she had begun weekly lessons from the vicar on understanding the Bible better.

It was a relief to know she was trying to understand him and his work.

Cameron then prayed for Claudia, that she would be safe on her voyage to America and that God would allow her to find a man to love and one who would adore her. "Help Claudia find happiness and peace, Lord. Help us all to find it," he prayed aloud, his voice soft as he looked up at the clear, cloudless sky.

"That is all any of us can ask, is it not?"

Hearing Aurora's voice startled Cameron from his prayer. Whirling around he saw her standing there watching him with troubled eyes.

"Aurora," he gasped, so stunned was he that she'd even

ventured down to this rough area of town. Then he remembered what he'd been saying in his prayer. Had she heard? "I was just—"

"You don't have to explain yourself, Cameron," she interrupted him quietly. "I did not mean to eavesdrop on your prayer. I've only come to tell you something."

She was acting quite out of character from her usual self. Normally she was smiling and animated when she saw him and kept up a constant stream of chatter about the wedding arrangements.

Something was definitely troubling her today. "Shall we sit down?" he asked, motioning toward a bench, but she shook her head.

"No. If I don't tell you this now, I may lose my nerve." She looked away and let out a long breath. "I lied about Lord Carmichael. Though Papa did urge me to find a husband, he never threatened to marry me to the old lord."

"I know," Cameron said.

Her eyes widened as she turned back to him. "You knew?"

Cameron shrugged. "I found out when I ran into Lord Carmichael in town two weeks ago. He had returned from the Continent after four months, where he'd met and married a lady from Spain."

Aurora's cheeks turned pink as she glanced away once more. "Why didn't you say anything to me about it?"

"It would only make you feel bad. We both have enough on our minds."

Aurora looked back at him. "After all I have done, you still consider my feelings?"

Cameron sighed and reached out to take her hands into his own. "Aurora, whether you meant for this engagement to happen or not, it is a reality. Neither of us can change that, so now we must do everything we can to make the most of it."

Aurora seemed to search his eyes a moment before stepping

back and removing her hands from his. "I can change it," she whispered so softly Cameron was not sure he had heard her right.

"I beg your pardon?"

"I said I can change it," she said louder and more confidently. "I can end this engagement."

Cameron could scarcely breathe, so stunned was he by her words. "And how would you accomplish this?"

"I have accepted another man's proposal of marriage. We are to elope at Gretna Green tonight," she stated matter-of-factly. Gretna Green was a village just over the Scottish border where couples from every class would often go to elope since banns were not required to be posted.

Cameron struggled to comprehend what she was saying. "But it will be social suicide for you and whomever you marry. You must know this!"

Aurora did not seem affected by his words. "It will not matter. I am marrying a gentleman farmer from my village, a Mr. John Miller. He has offered many times for my hand, but I refused since I was hoping that—well—you know what I wanted," she explained, only faltering on those last words. "I wrote him two days ago and asked if he was still interested. He came to see me this morning and said he was. My only stipulation was that we elope, and he agreed to it."

Cameron studied the determined look on Aurora's face and still could not believe she was serious. Not after all she'd done to assure the engagement would happen. "Why, Aurora? Why are you doing this?"

She lowered her gaze. "Because I have recently become aware of my selfishness, and I am deeply ashamed of it." She brought her eyes back to his again. "All my life I have thought only of myself and what I could do or have. I wanted you, and so I set out to get you. I ridiculed your religious ways and scoffed at your wanting to help the poor. I wanted you to focus on me and nothing else."

"Aurora, we are all selfish at one time or an—"

"Yes, but I am that way all the time," she interrupted. "And that is why I have to do this. I came by the shelter a few days ago to see why you spent so much time here and to convince you to give it up. As my driver and I neared the shelter, I have to tell you I was appalled at how poor this area is. All I could think of was what the ton would say if they knew you came down here every day and mingled with the riffraff of the city." She paused and walked over to look down at the river.

Cameron watched her and found he felt let down by her remarks. Of course he knew every other young lady in London would have the same feelings, but a part of him had hoped she would try to understand.

Aurora continued after a pause. "I walked in and saw all those ragged-looking women and children and shuddered when one of the little ones brushed up against my skirt. I immediately judged them all unworthy even to be in my presence and set off down the hall to look for your office."

Cameron had walked over to stand by her while she spoke. He wanted to defend his work and the people he helped every day but felt God telling him to wait. He knew he must hear the rest. "Was I not there?" he prompted when she hesitated again.

She looked up at him and nodded. "Yes, but I ran into someone before I could find you, and I have to tell you I was even more appalled at her presence than I was about anything else I'd seen that morning."

Cameron knew right away who she was talking about. "You saw Claudia."

She gave him a small smile. "Don't look so worried, Cameron. Yes, I saw her, and I accused her of trying to steal you away from me, which she promptly denied."

Cameron hadn't seen Claudia since the day she quit the

shelter, and he could only imagine how speaking to Aurora affected her. "Aurora, you know I would not play you false no matter what the circumstances of our engagement."

She held out her hand as if to stop his defense. "I know, Cameron. I was just surprised at seeing her there. But now I'm glad I did." She turned once more to the water. "When I told her I wanted you to give up the shelter, she accused me of not really knowing you. She told me about your love for God and how you only desired to do His will. It was like someone had opened a curtain, and suddenly I saw things I never had before."

"These are things I've told you already, Aurora," he gently reminded her.

"But I never heard them, Cam. Claudia so passionately defended you, and I suppose I was shamed by the fact that I had to be told these things by the woman who lost you to me."

"Aurora, please don't—"

"Say the truth?" she interjected. "You love Claudia, and she loves you. She is the one you want to marry, and I don't blame you. She wants the same things in her life as you do." Reaching inside her satin purse, Aurora pulled out his grandmother's ring and handed it to him. "She is the one who needs to wear this ring."

Cameron slowly reached out and took the jewel-encrusted ring from her. Hope bloomed in his heart; yet it was warring with concern for Aurora. "Are you sure about this, Aurora? Is John Miller a man with whom you can live your life?"

She smiled sadly at him. "I am not being totally unselfish in this decision, you know. I like John, and I know he loves me despite all my flaws and will do everything he can to make my life a happy one. He has always been that way to me, but I wouldn't accept it until now." She reached out her hand and cupped his cheek. "Be well, Cameron," she whispered and turned to walk away.

"Thank you, Aurora," he said, watching her leave. As his thumb caressed the smooth underside of the ring, his mind raced with thoughts of what to do next.

And then he knew. Tucking the ring safely in his pocket, Cameron headed for the shelter. He had a lot of arrangements to make, favors to call in, and people to speak to, if he was going to make his plan work.

❧

The next morning Claudia arrived at the dock and, after bidding a tearful Helen good-bye, bravely boarded the ship that would be taking her back home to her family and away from Cameron.

The captain's wife, Mrs. O'Leary, was the first to greet her and welcome her aboard. Claudia could tell she and the kind older woman would get along well. After she showed Claudia to her room and helped her put away some of her things, Mrs. O'Leary explained about the schedule of the meals and introduced her to a maid who would personally assist her during the voyage.

Finally Mrs. O'Leary glanced at the watch pinned to her blouse. "Well, my lady, we'll be leaving port soon, so I'd better be checkin' with my husband to see if he needs me for anythin'. Remember your maid is right next door to ye, so just give the cord here a little tug if you'll be needin' somethin' and she'll come runnin'," Mrs. O'Leary informed her in her soft Irish brogue, while pointing out the scarlet cord next to the vanity.

"Thank you, Mrs. O'Leary. I'm sure I'll be fine," Claudia assured her.

After the captain's wife had left, Claudia glanced about her small cabin and already began to feel the pangs of loneliness engulf her. She walked over to her bed and sat down on the edge with a long sigh. *Am I doing the right thing?* she wondered. *Or am I just running away?*

Looking up at the beamed ceiling, she thought of all the

prayers she'd prayed over the last few weeks and the scriptures she'd read and found comfort in. She especially held on to the one that said the joy of the Lord was her strength. The vicar had told her joy didn't mean happiness, but it meant having every confidence that God was with her at all times to see her through every trial.

He knew her pain and knew she desired to be that happy, carefree woman she'd been before Helen's ball. Oddly, praying for Cameron and Aurora seemed to help her better accept her circumstances. She truly did hope their marriage would be happy and that his shelter would continue to flourish and meet the needs of more and more women and children.

One day, perhaps, she would be able to be friends with them, and their relationship would be reflected upon as a fond and distant memory.

At least she prayed it would be so.

A knock on her door startled her out of her musings. Thinking it must be either the maid or Mrs. O'Leary, she opened it, not checking to see who it was first.

She was staggered when she saw who stood there.

"Cameron!" she gasped, her eyes scanning him from head to toe as if to assure herself it was really he. He seemed extraordinarily handsome standing there in his grey vest and black pants and Hessians, smiling at her. His black cape was thrown rakishly over one shoulder, and she reflected that he looked much like Jean Lafitte had that time she'd met him. "What are you doing here?"

He reached out and took her hand, pulling her out into the hallway. "I'm not marrying Aurora," he told her, shocking her even further. "She broke our engagement and has decided to marry someone else!"

Claudia could hardly believe her ears as he explained his and Aurora's ending conversation. "But—the wedding—your guests!" she stammered.

"Aurora posted the cancellation in the *Times* yesterday," he assured her. Still holding on to her hand, he brought it to his lips and kissed it tenderly. "We have been granted a miracle, Claude, and I'm sorry if I am making an incorrect assumption of your feelings. But I was not going to waste another minute."

Claudia's heart sped up even faster at the implication of his words. "Your assumptions are not incorrect. My feelings are as they always were," she assured him breathlessly.

His eyes softened as they searched her own. "I was afraid—" He paused and let out a breath. "Then you forgive me for not dealing with Aurora sooner? Had I not promised her I—"

She put her finger over his lips stopping him. "There is nothing to forgive, Cameron. You could not know what would happen. You must forgive yourse—" The ship swayed then, reminding Claudia of where they were. "Oh, no! The ship was readying to sail just now. We must get off, or else our reputations will be ruined forever."

She started to turn toward the stairs that would take them up on deck, but he wouldn't let go of her hand. "Wait, Claudia. It's completely all right." He reached in his vest and pulled out an official document. "I was able to get us a special license. Let's go right now and let the captain marry us!"

Claudia was so surprised that she merely stared at the license as if it were a foreign object.

Then she realized what he was trying to say to her. "You want to get married? Now?"

He chuckled and tucked it back into his vest. "I know it's a bit hasty, but I don't want to risk anything or anyone else coming between us."

She shook her head and glanced down at her plain gray traveling dress. "But this is not what I'd imagined I would wear on my wedding day. And what about my grandfathers and—and your family. You know your mother will be furious if we—"

"Claude!" Cameron exclaimed softly, cupping both her cheeks gently. "Do you love me?"

Claudia looked into the deep green of his eyes and saw her own feelings reflected there. "Yes," she whispered breathlessly. "I do love you, Cameron."

"And I love you, Claudia," he declared in a low voice while his thumb caressed her cheek. "I want you to be my wife. I want us to dream together and do the work of the Lord side by side. I want us to have babies with your eyes and see them bounced on their Grandpa George's knee."

Tears filled Claudia's eyes as she envisioned his beautifully spoken words. "I'd like that, too."

"Then marry me, Claudia. Today, in your gray dress and ribbon-less bonnet." He teased with a grin, but then his expression turned very serious. "I don't want to spend another day without you."

How could she resist that? "All right, I'll marry you."

With a triumphant smile he reached inside his coat pocket and took out his grandmother's ring. After slipping it on her finger he bent to kiss it. "I had planned to give you this ring the night of your ball."

Claudia's gaze flew from the sparkling ring to his eyes. "I had wondered. . . ," she murmured. "Helen had said that was what you wanted but—"

He leaned forward and kissed her so gently and sweetly that she didn't open her eyes for a few moments, even after he'd stopped. When she finally did look at him, he was smiling at her.

"Do you know that every time you've kissed me, you've interrupted me in midsentence?" she said, her head still spinning a little from the kiss.

He thought a moment. "You know, I believe you are right. Odd, that!"

She narrowed her eyes at him with a mock frown. "Are you trying to say I talk too much?"

He bent to give her another quick kiss. "Absolutely not. It's just that I am too impatient to wait until you are finished talking to act on my feelings." He grinned at her and pointed toward the deck. "Well, shall we go to the captain and bind our lives together forever?"

She threaded her arm through his. "Absolutely. Lead on!"

They both chuckled as he led her up to the top deck. She was about to ask him why he thought the captain would be there when something else caught her eye.

There crowded on the deck were her grandfathers, Helen and North, and Cameron's parents and sisters.

"What—," she started to ask but couldn't find the words as they all looked their way.

"It is a good thing you agreed to marry me, or else all these people would leave sorely disappointed," Cameron whispered to her, leading her to them. "You have a choice. After the ceremony we can disembark with everyone else, or we can sail and visit your parents. I am ready for either."

She looked up at him and thanked God again for leading Cameron back to her. "I'd like my parents to meet you," she said without having to think about it too much.

Cameron put his other hand over the one on his arm. "Then that is what we shall do."

They greeted the captain, and as he was instructing them where to stand, Cameron's mother came rushing up to them.

"Oh, Cameron, must you forever break my heart with such unconventional ways of doing things?" She dabbed at her eyes and sniffed daintily. "What will everyone say when they hear you did not marry in a church? And what happened between you and Aurora? Did you know she has eloped with a *farmer*?" She quickly looked at Claudia and said, "I mean no disrespect to you, dear. But the entire ton will be abuzz with gossip, and I promise none of it will be pleasant."

"Mother, if I pledge to you we will have our marriage

blessed in a church on our return from America, will you *please* let us continue?" Cameron asked, clearly anxious to get on with the ceremony.

"What?" she gasped, clutching her handkerchief to her chest. "You are bound for the colonies? And what other secrets am I to discover today? I cannot believe—"

"Margaret!" his father called out as he walked up and seized his wife's arm. "You can scold him later. Can't you see the poor boy is eager to marry?" He tugged her away.

"Shall we begin?" the captain said, bringing her attention back to Cameron and their ceremony.

As she and Cameron exchanged their vows in front of their family and friends, Claudia couldn't take her eyes off the man she had believed she'd lost forever. Gazing at him, reciting the words to love, honor, and cherish, out on the sea with the beautiful blue sky as their canopy, felt so appropriate. She could even imagine God looking down upon them and smiling.

As they neared the end of the ceremony, Claudia was thankful Cameron waited until the captain had given him a cue to kiss her, instead of interrupting her vows. She heard a ripple of sighs as he kissed her gently and then placed another one on her cheek in a loving gesture.

Once the captain announced they were man and wife, Helen hurriedly stepped forward to hug her. "Before you ask, I did not know about this until we'd walked back to our carriage and were met by Lord Kinclary!" Helen stood back and beamed at her. "But isn't this the most romantic gesture you've ever beheld!"

Claudia laughed. "Undeniably the most!" she agreed, and then the reality of it all seemed to rush back to her. "Can you believe it, Helen? I am married to Cameron!"

"If I did not witness the wedding I would not believe it!" she said with a grin. "So, *Lady Kinclary!* Will you be going to Louisiana after all?"

"Yes, but don't worry. It will be a quick visit to see my parents and to show Cameron my home. We will come back to England in no time at all."

Helen sighed and then smiled tearfully at her. "Please give my regards to your parents and sister!"

Claudia assured her she would and hugged her one more time.

Because the captain was in a hurry to set sail, she was only able to say quick good-byes before everyone had to disembark.

They stood on the starboard bow and scanned the shore as the ship slowly drew further and further away. They waved to Helen and North who stood watching them from the pier.

"Helen told me how God had brought her and North together by quite miraculous means," she mentioned as they stood there, arm in arm, with the sea air blowing their garments and hair.

Cameron nodded. "Perhaps, like them, we will appreciate each other more since we went through so much to be together."

She looked at his handsome profile, and her heart swelled even more. "Have I told you yet, Cameron Montbatten, that I love you with all my heart?"

He looked at her and appeared to be thinking on her words. "Yes, but I think I should like to hear it again."

"I love you," she whispered to him.

Cameron looked at her and shook his head. "I'm sorry, but I couldn't hear that."

She narrowed her eyes. "I love you," she said a little louder.

He cocked his head to the side as if trying to hear her better. "No. No, I'm sorry, but I still didn't hear you."

Claudia rolled her eyes. "I love you!" she then declared as loudly as she looked out to the sea.

Cameron glanced around, and when she followed his gaze she noticed the crew and a few of the passengers had stopped to stare at them. "Well done, my dear. Now everyone can be certain as to where your feelings lie."

Claudia covered her face and groaned. "Oh, no."

"There is only one course of action to take now." She was about to ask what action that was when he swooped down and kissed her right on the lips.

"Cameron!" she gasped, breaking the kiss and leaning away from him. "Everyone is watching."

"Yes, but there it is. After hearing your words of love I had to do *something*."

She giggled and peeked about to see that only a few were watching them now. "You are a gentleman. And gentlemen do not go about kissing their ladies in public. It is not the *done thing*," she scolded because she felt she needed to. But then she confessed, "It was your first kiss, though, that made me realize I did have feelings for you."

His brows rose in surprise. "But you seemed quite vexed with me. And, as I recall, you delivered a slap that kept my ears ringing for days."

"I've already explained it was my duty to slap you, whether I liked the kiss or not."

He nodded as if it all made perfect sense. "Right you are, my dear. I expected no less."

He put his arms around her and held her back to his chest as they continued to watch the shrinking buildings of London. "I still can hardly believe you are in my arms, Claude. Just thinking of all we've been through, I feel I'm truly a blessed man," he said after a long moment, his voice solemn and humble.

Closing her eyes, she leaned back against him and felt him place a gentle kiss on her head. *We're both blessed,* she thought.

And to think it all started with a kiss. . . .

A Letter To Our Readers

Dear Reader:
In order that we might better contribute to your reading enjoyment, we would appreciate your taking a few minutes to respond to the following questions. We welcome your comments and read each form and letter we receive. When completed, please return to the following:

Fiction Editor
Heartsong Presents
PO Box 719
Uhrichsville, Ohio 44683

1. Did you enjoy reading *A Gentleman's Kiss* by Kimberley Comeaux?
   ❏ Very much! I would like to see more books by this author!
   ❏ Moderately. I would have enjoyed it more if

   _____

   _____

   _____

2. Are you a member of **Heartsong Presents**?   ❏ Yes   ❏ No
   If no, where did you purchase this book? _____

   _____

3. How would you rate, on a scale from 1 (poor) to 5 (superior), the cover design? _____

4. On a scale from 1 (poor) to 10 (superior), please rate the following elements.

   ____ Heroine   ____ Plot
   ____ Hero   ____ Inspirational theme
   ____ Setting   ____ Secondary characters

5. These characters were special because? _____
_____
_____

6. How has this book inspired your life? _____
_____
_____

7. What settings would you like to see covered in future
   Heartsong Presents books? _____
_____
_____

8. What are some inspirational themes you would like to see
   treated in future books? _____
_____
_____

9. Would you be interested in reading other **Heartsong
   Presents** titles? ❑ Yes ❑ No

10. Please check your age range:
   ❑ Under 18   ❑ 18-24
   ❑ 25-34   ❑ 35-45
   ❑ 46-55   ❑ Over 55

Name _____
Occupation _____
Address _____
City, State, Zip _____

Heart♥ng

HEARTSONG PRESENTS TITLES AVAILABLE NOW:

Presents

Great Inspirational Romance at a Great Price!

Heartsong Presents books are inspirational romances in
contemporary and historical settings, designed to give you an
enjoyable, spirit-lifting reading experience. You can choose
wonderfully written titles from some of today's best authors like
Peggy Darty, Sally Laity, DiAnn Mills, Colleen L. Reece,
Debra White Smith, and many others.

When ordering quantities less than twelve, above titles are $2.97 each.
Not all titles may be available at time of order.

SEND TO: **Heartsong Presents** Reader's Service
P.O. Box 721, Uhrichsville, Ohio 44683

Please send me the items checked above. I am enclosing $ _____
(please add $2.00 to cover postage per order. OH add 7% tax. NJ
add 6%). Send check or money order, no cash or C.O.D.s, please.

To place a credit card order, call 1-740-922-7280.

NAME _____

ADDRESS _____

CITY/STATE _____ ZIP_____

HPS 3-06

HEARTSONG
P R E S E N T S

If you love Christian romance…

$10.99

You'll love Heartsong Presents' inspiring and faith-filled romances by today's very best Christian authors…DiAnn Mills, Wanda E. Brunstetter, and Yvonne Lehman, to mention a few!

When you join Heartsong Presents, you'll enjoy four brand-new, mass market, 176-page books—two contemporary and two historical—that will build you up in your faith when you discover God's role in every relationship you read about!

Imagine…four new romances every four weeks—with men and women like you who long to meet the one God has chosen as the love of their lives…all for the low price of $10.99 postpaid.

Mass Market 176 Pages

To join, simply visit www.heartsong presents.com or complete the coupon below and mail it to the address provided.

✄- -

YES! Sign me up for Heart♥ng!

NEW MEMBERSHIPS WILL BE SHIPPED IMMEDIATELY!
Send no money now. We'll bill you only $10.99 postpaid with your first shipment of four books. Or for faster action, call 1-740-922-7280.

NAME_____

ADDRESS_____

CITY_____ STATE _____ ZIP _____

MAIL TO: HEARTSONG PRESENTS, P.O. Box 721, Uhrichsville, Ohio 44683
or sign up at WWW.HEARTSONGPRESENTS.COM